Just A Summer Girl

Helen Cavanagh

SCHOLASTIC INC.
New York Toronto London Auckland Sydney Tokyo

For my nieces: Laurel, Marla, & Joni—
who will always be summer girls.

Cover Photo by Owen Brown

ISBN 0-590-31962-0

13 12 11 10 9 8 7 6 5 4 3 2   3 4 5 6 7/8

Printed in the U.S.A.   06

Just A
Summer Girl

A Wildfire Book

WILDFIRE TITLES
FROM SCHOLASTIC

Chapter
— *One* —

Weeks before Miss Lowell's Private School for Girls lets out for the summer, I'm ready. This year, by the time the calendar made summer official on June twenty-first, I was so ready I was almost screaming, "Beach! Beach!" For the next three days, until Dad was able to leave for his vacation, every conversation in our house seemed to begin: "When we get to Grantham . . ."

So wouldn't you think I'd be glad that Dad insisted on leaving at the crack of dawn? I wasn't; I could barely keep my eyes open. As we packed the car and locked the front door of our townhouse on Beacon Hill, and even as we headed out of Boston and hit Storrow Drive, I kept yawning and protesting. But then, settled in the backseat of the car, surrounded by pillows and boxes, I began to smile. We were on our way to Grantham. Finally.

Mom was very excited. She kept bouncing

around in the front seat, smiling first at Dad, then turning to smile at me. Dad never stopped smiling, or humming. I was smiling, too, when I wasn't dozing. Anyone passing us in another car must have thought we were a bunch of grinning idiots. After a while I really dozed off, but Mom poked me awake when we were crossing the Bourne Bridge.

"Look how the sun hits the water, Nina," she said, sighing. "We couldn't have a better day, could we?"

We really couldn't. It was a perfect, sunshiny morning. The silky blue water far below us seemed stitched all over with golden sequins of sun.

I dozed off again until Dad's announcement: "Grantham — next exit."

After that there was no sleeping for me. The exit leads to a windy, bumpy access road past Brickhouse Pond and Tucker's Airport. Then we turned left onto Route 6. That's the road that leads straight to Grantham, straight to summer.

Entering Grantham, we passed the starchyneat Methodist Church, and then the tiny triangle of grass that doubles as a traffic island and a standing place for the huge statue of Josiah Grantham. Mom waved to the founding father and blew him a kiss, as she does every year.

"Hi there, Tall, Gaunt, and Granite," she said in her most flirtatious voice.

Dad let out a deafening yell and threw off his old white golf hat.

2

"We're here — yippee!"

At that moment, Dad was definitely not Whitney Burnham Hale, Attorney-at-Law; he was an eager, shiny-eyed little boy. He rolled down the window on his side, stuck out his head, and inhaled deeply. I don't think Dad is ever really not happy, but now he was very happy.

He loves Grantham and so do I. I love summer. I loved that we were together and all feeling so good. I missed my sister Nicole, who is married now and was not here to share the backseat and that moment with me. But I still had Mom and Dad and one more summer in Grantham. I couldn't wait to see everyone.

Now I was glad Dad made us leave so early; it was still breakfast time. We would have it at Tucker's Inn, of course — cranberry muffins right out of the oven, bacon and eggs, and if Dad could persuade someone to heat and serve it so early, a bowl of quahog chowder, buttery sweet, milky hot. Quahogs are like clams — only, I think, better.

The waitress was the first to say it: "Well now, folks, down for the summer?"

Down for the summer, *down* the Cape. There are arguments about that. Some people insist they drive *up* to the Cape and *down* to Maine. Maybe they're right, but we wouldn't dream of saying anything but "going up to Maine" and "down the Cape." And what we were now "officially" was *down for the summer.*

I was happy with my hot buttery muffin, and

when Mom took her first spoonful of chowder I was afraid she was going to pass out from pleasure.

"Don't anyone talk to me," she murmured. "I think I just died and went to heaven."

I thought again, This is my last summer, and I got a funny feeling — sad. But of course it wouldn't really be my last — that's exaggerating. Yes, I'll be in Paris next summer, but after that — lots of summers after that — I'll be free to return to Grantham-by-the-Sea.

That's what it says on the huge Chamber of Commerce sign — GRANTHAM-BY-THE-SEA, CAPE COD'S PRETTIEST TOWN, STAY AND SEE. Falmouth, Dennis, Harwich, Chatham, Orleans are pretty, too; but I agreed with the sign — Grantham is the prettiest, the best.

But of course I'm prejudiced, and so is Dad. He's been coming here since he was a little baby. His boyhood summer home is now our home since Grandma and Grandpa Hale died. Nicole and I took our first steps on Tucker's Beach, and Mom says I ate enough sand to qualify to be a beach myself.

Funny, though. The Hales have been coming to Grantham for years — generations — and we're still considered newcomers by the local people. We call them "Capies" and they call us "summer people." It's almost a law: If you weren't born in Grantham, if you don't live here all year round, then you're treated in that polite but peculiar way reserved for paying customers. It seems silly to me that there should be such a sharp distinction between us —

Capies and non-Capies — but that's how it is, no exceptions.

Therefore, I am now officially a summer girl. I knew I would be hearing that a lot now.

I didn't have to wait long. After breakfast, and after we had opened the house, unpacked the car, and put things away, I walked back to town. My first stop was Webb's Pharmacy & Essentials. I was paying for my first bottle of suntan oil and the nicely fat bonus fiction issue of *Seventeen* when I heard it.

"Ayuh, love to see you summer girls start comin' in here, yessir. Brightens up the place, donchaknow?"

Mr. Webb took my money, and the fluorescent light bouncing off his glasses made it seem like he was beaming at me. He did have a big smile on his face but I could sense — I knew that it wasn't a real smile. He never remembers my name. To him I am just one of many summer girls.

"Good to see you," he said. "Down for the summer now?"

He answered himself.

"Ayuh, that's fine. Love to see you summer girls."

"Thank you, Mr. Webb," I said politely. "It's great to be here."

He had no trouble agreeing with that.

"Ayuh."

So to the people who call Grantham home all year round, I am not Nina Hale, sixteen years old with medium length dark blond hair, hazel eyes that turn green, and three tiny moles

5

(beauty marks) arranged in a triangle on my left cheek. (Nicole calls it my equilateral mole.) No, to the locals I am not a real person, not an individual. It's as if I am just one kernel on an ear of corn or something.

Oh, well. Besides, I never felt like an alien when my friends arrived: John Carlton, Bunny Sutherland, Sandi Howard, Ross Bradford, Amy Sears. It was possible they would all get down that day, if not at least by the next. Then summer would really begin for me.

On the way home I couldn't resist stopping at Pate's Cove. The cove is my favorite place: tiny, just a dune or two, a protected little scoop of sand where I can go to be alone or to sketch or paint. I was planning to do a whole series of cove studies this summer, in all media: pen and ink, pastel, watercolor, oil. This would be my last chance to do it for a while; next summer, right after graduation from Miss Lowell's I'd be going to Paris, a whole new world for me to capture on canvas. I couldn't wait!

What was I saying? I *could* wait! I was really looking forward to this summer, and there were lots of new techniques I needed to master. Gemma Russell, my art teacher, does not believe in vacations for artists.

"Day or night, awake or dreaming, you will always be the artist; nothing should be wasted. You are either an artist or a pretender."

Miss Russell is very, very sparing with compliments, but this year she broke down and told me: "Yes, Nina, by all means go to Paris.

6

You must find every opportunity for yourself because you are burdened with a real talent."

Up until that moment, I was never sure she even liked my work; the only signs of approval were the funny little noises she made in her throat, like a cat's purr. And *burdened* with talent. Such a strange word to use. Gemma Russell is kind of a strange person, too, a one-of-a-kind. She's taught me so much. I like her a lot.

The sun was really shining now, hot. I took off my sandals and walked closer to the water. The ocean was calm, the incoming waves mild ripples, but the water slapping against my toes was cold, cold. I endured it, though — willingly — because I love it. In a week or so, the water would be warmer, after the sun had a chance to work on it. And my hair would be just the way I like it best, sun-streaked, salty-thick — my summer hair. And my pale winter skin would change and transform me. I tan easily.

Then I saw him.

He stood at the very end of the long wharf, and as I watched, he bent over, picked up a barrel, and dumped its contents into the water. Seagulls, pushy and screaming, flew to the scene. Even from far away I could see his teeth flash in a broad grin as he waved his arms at the birds. I raised my arm and used my hand as a visor so I could see him better.

He had dark hair, straight — and too long, I thought. And he was very tall, and probably too skinny. No, I decided a second later, not skinny — lean.

I couldn't stop looking. There was something about him that made my cheeks heat up and my throat go dry. The water seemed to change instantly; my feet, icy cold, were now deliciously warm. I stood there like a statue, staring, waiting.

Waiting? For what, I wondered. He hadn't noticed me. I didn't know him and he didn't know me, and as I watched him walk back toward Pate's Fish Shack at the land's end of the wharf, it occurred to me that I would probably never see him again.

Then he did notice me. He was using his hand as a visor, too, looking straight at me. It seemed as though I could feel his gaze, intense, and warmer than the sun that was beating down on my shoulders.

I couldn't just stand there staring. I turned and walked away, not letting myself turn around and look back once.

But all the way home I thought about him. I wondered who he was, where he lived. Could this be his first summer in Grantham? Maybe his family bought one of those new houses we saw going up at the end of last summer. Dad had absolutely hated those redwood and glass houses.

"Too modern — tacky. Not Grantham at all."

Dad hates it when anyone tampers with the traditional, colonial style that is truly Cape Cod.

I had so many questions about the boy on the

wharf. Boy? He seemed so tall, graceful, *older*. What did he look like up close? Maybe he's only gorgeous from a distance, I thought. Very possible.

The minute I got home, I had to put all my wonderings aside. Sandy, John, Bunny, and Amy were all sitting on my porch waiting for me. We jumped around like fiends, as if we hadn't just seen each other a few days ago in Boston. We were excited, though, because we were down for the summer together.

"Ross will be down today, too," Sandi said. "My mother talked to his mother yesterday."

I laughed. "Good old Ross. Wonder what he's been up to this year? Something outrageous, probably. I can't wait to hear his this year's stories, can you?"

Ross Bradford is a character, *our* character — a real clown, a daredevil. In February, when I got a huge valentine in the mail signed only, "Guess Who?" I knew immediately it was Ross who sent it, even before I checked the postmark: Andover, Massachusetts. Ross goes to Phillips Academy. Unless he got kicked out. Oh, he's really not that bad, but he does love his practical jokes. For such a little guy — short, wiry, too skinny — Ross has big ideas and big nerve.

"Second show tonight, everybody?" John's eyes were magnified mischief behind his thick glasses. "Guess what's playing."

Sandi and I exchanged glances and groaned together.

"We *know* what's playing, John," I said.

9

"Even if I hadn't seen the marquee when we drove past this morning, I'd know what movie is playing," Sandi said, laughing. "The first movie of the summer, the first movie ever made, the longest movie — "

John interrupted her. "Maybe the longest movie, Sandi, but *Gone with the Wind* isn't the first."

John knows everything so we both know not to argue, but *GWTW* is always the first movie of the summer, another Grantham tradition. It would help if they would invest in some comfortable seats, though. By the end of fifteen minutes, *my* seat always falls asleep. It would be murder tonight.

We wouldn't think of not going to the movies on our first night. The second show is where you get to see everyone.

"I hear Ross has changed a lot," Amy was saying. "I haven't seen him, but my friend Muffy goes out with his roommate, and Muffy says Ross is a knockout."

We all laughed unbelievingly, even John. *Ross?*

"You probably have it all wrong, Amy," Sandi said. "Your friend Muffy probably meant that Ross knocked out a wall, or maybe even her boyfriend."

John shook his head. "Uh uh, Ross is definitely not the violent type."

I had to agree with that. Ross is cute, if you like the bratty little brother type. My mother used to call him Dennis the Menace. He even looks like the cartoon character, a thatch of straw-colored hair and an impudent, laughing face. Still, it would be good to see him again; he never failed to liven things up.

After that we decided to walk to the Yacht Club beach, and we fooled around there until late afternoon. The beach was almost empty, but I knew that wouldn't last long. By the weekend the club would be summer-busy — all the little kids, their baby-sitters, their parents, and all the elderly club members would be there. The big bright umbrellas were lined up against the fence that separated the Yacht Club from the public beach, and the tables and lounge chairs all had a new coat of gleaming white paint.

Amy checked out this season's lifeguards, and she sighed, disappointed.

"They could have hired someone gorgeous. I mean, would it have killed them?"

Sandi and I looked at her and then at each other and shrugged. Amy said the same thing every year.

I was dying to tell Sandi about the boy on the wharf, but there was always someone else there with us. I didn't want to share him with anyone except Sandi yet.

When we left the beach and headed for home I did have a few minutes alone with her, but she had something to talk about.

"John's still in love with Amy, isn't he, Nina?" she asked with a glum expression.

She didn't seem to expect an answer, though, thank heavens.

"I'm going to make him notice *me* this sum-

11

mer," she said. "I don't know how, but I'm going to try. He's such a dope about Amy . . . I mean, will he ever learn? I know he's intelligent — the most intelligent boy I know — but he's not very smart about women."

John Carlton has had eyes only for Amy since fifth grade. She couldn't care less, although she's just nice enough to him so that he keeps on hoping. He leaves Grantham every September still loving her and planning how they can see each other during the winter. I don't know how Amy manages to keep him on the string but she does. Sandi was right. John just doesn't see Amy very clearly, and it's not because of the fact that he wears glasses for his poor eyesight. John has never, ever given Sandi more than an old-buddy, good-pal glance.

I wanted to cheer her up. "Maybe this summer will be different," I said. "You never know, San."

We parted then, and when I reached my house, Mom was fixing a salad and Dad was out on the patio at the grill turning steaks. I set the table and we all chattered happily. What was there not to be happy about?

After dinner I went upstairs and took a long shower. I dressed carefully but casually in my favorite blue-and-white striped boy's shirt and white jeans. I knotted the sleeves of a baby blue crewneck sweater around my neck. One day of hot sun had given me lots of color. I'd lost my wan, winter look; I looked healthier and, I thought, prettier. Without a tan, and especially during the longest, dreariest months of the year — February and March — I get unhappy with the way I look, so pale and faded. Usually, though, I'm so involved with school, and then after school with my art, that I don't much care. I mean, there's a lot of satisfaction in putting just the right colors in my paintings. Dad gets a big kick, though, when I come downstairs after a long session at my easel with smudges of oil paint — burnt sienna, prussian blue, vermilion — all over my face. I guess, then, you could call *that* look my winter look.

But tonight the way I looked mattered. Maybe the boy on the wharf would be going to the movies, too, or walking around Grantham. Having a coat of tan — that special glow — made me feel better, maybe even my best.

Probably I'd never see him again. Even if I did, maybe I wouldn't be interested at all. Yet I couldn't stop thinking about him, couldn't turn off the picture of him that kept flashing in my mind: dark, lean, the gleam of his smile, the graceful way he moved. He'd made a nice picture there on the wharf; maybe it was just that he appealed to my "artist's eye." That happens often. I see someone — a face in the crowd, a person sitting on a bench in the Boston Public Garden, a little boy feeding the pigeons, and I wish I could freeze them into position, paint them, capture them on canvas just because I find them appealing, beautiful. Maybe that's what it was with the tall boy on the wharf that afternoon.

Anyway, I decided I wouldn't say anything to Sandi until I'd had another look. I also decided that I'd go early to the cove the next morning.

I gave my hair one last comb with my fingers and smiled at myself in the mirror.

"Tomorrow," I said out loud. I felt so happy — that peaceful feeling I get when everything is right and good things are still ahead. That's what I liked. It was only the beginning of summer. I had lots of tomorrows.

Chapter Two

"Hi there, Nina — it's really good to see you."

Ross Bradford, crowd clown, good friend, fun person — the last person in the world I would consider a boyfriend — stood there smiling at me. His straw-yellow hair was tamed, neat, and nicely cut, and his face was thinner or longer or something. He looked years older, *better*. Okay, he was handsome.

"Hi, Ross. When did you get down?"

He looked down at me. "About an hour ago. Just in time."

The *way* he was looking at me.

"Right," I said. "Now you won't miss your old girlfriend, Scarlett O'Hara."

Ross had always made loud kissing noises during the movie and then acted innocent when the ushers tried to eject him from the movie theater.

He didn't laugh, just kept looking at me, and

finally he grinned and said very softly, "Right, now I won't miss my old girlfriend."

Could this tall, good-looking boy really be Ross Bradford? Dennis the Menace?

Everyone started arriving then, and we chatted on my porch, waiting for the only straggler, Bunny.

"Bunny better get hopping," John said, and we all laughed automatically. Old joke.

Sandi nudged me when Ross had turned to talk to John.

"Are you checking that out, Neens? I mean, can you believe him?"

I shook my head.

"Amy's friend was right," she said. "Ross is a knockout."

I nodded and whispered. "And *tall*. *I* can't believe how tall."

He had grown at least half a foot during the winter, if that's possible. It was hard to believe that this was the same boy who set off fire-crackers in Webb's Pharmacy on a Sunday morning and stuffed jellyfish in his mother's beach bag. He had made Yacht Club history the night he dumped his "special" ice cubes in the punch bowl at the Labor Day Dance two years ago. Ross had collected a couple of dozen tiny sand crabs and froze them in ice cube trays. Miraculously, when they thawed, they came to life and crawled away. At least, no one could find them in the morning, and with no evidence, Ross escaped serious punishment. As a matter of fact, the older club members still laugh about it.

Bunny Sutherland sauntered across the lawn, stopping once to comb her hair and then again to adjust her belt.

We all looked at each other and groaned.

"She is definitely not hopping," Sandi said.

"She never does," I said. "Has Bunny ever been on time for anything?"

I noticed we were all smiling at her, though — fondly. Bunny is a really sweet girl, and if she is not exactly punctual or dependable, that's her only fault.

"I guess I fell asleep," she said when she reached the porch. "I didn't miss anything, did I?"

Then she noticed Ross, gave him a big hello, and as she did, I saw the way her eyes widened. Sandi and I weren't the only ones checking out the "new" Ross Bradford.

Amy, too. Amy was practically pushing John off the porch trying to get in position beside Ross. Hmmm-mm.

Then John made the first move. "Come on, you guys, let's get gone with the wind."

We all followed him, happily, except Amy. She groaned.

"I don't know if I can't stand sitting through that movie again. Do we have to stay to the end?"

No one answered her. Amy always says that. Anyway, it isn't the movie that's playing that is important; it's the lining up out in front of the dinky little theater on Main Street, having a chance to look everyone over, and let everyone look us over. The movie changes once a week, and every week we're all there. It's part of a Grantham summer — we wouldn't have missed it for anything.

The one boy I wanted to see wasn't there, so I tried to concentrate on Ross, which wasn't too hard because he was so nice to me. I wouldn't have been normal if I wasn't flattered by his attention.

I realized that Ross hadn't called me Nee, not even once. This summer I was Nina.

That was an old joke, too. Ross said, when I was about twelve, that the first thing anyone would notice about me was my "notably knobby knees." "They knock when you walk," he said, and then laughed like a maniac. Ever since he has called me Nee or NeeNee, and Sandi calls me Neens.

Now he was calling me Nina, and when he looked at me, there was an expression on his face that reminded me of the way John looks at Amy.

We did stay for the end of the movie; we decided we needed to hear Scarlett getting told off again: "Frankly, my dear, I don't give a damn." After that, we decided we definitely needed food, and we headed for (where else?) The Sou'wester.

At the movies I sat between Sandi and Bunny, but when we got to the restaurant I had to notice the effort Ross made to sit beside me in the booth. Sandi noticed, too; that girl doesn't miss very much.

"Oh, oh," she hissed in my ear, "watch out."

I shot her a hush-up look with my eyes, and she just grinned devilishly.

Ross was sitting very close to me. Of course, he couldn't help that; we all crammed in one small wooden booth.

"So tell me. How was your year? Did you get any interesting mail, for instance?"

He wore that old mischievous look, and I laughed.

"Not much," I said. "Unless you want to count one monster valentine that I had to pay the postage due for." I made a clucking sound. "*Some* people."

My voice was as light and teasing as I could make it, but I felt shy with him, different. He's almost a stranger, I thought.

"And how was *your* year?"

"I graduated," he said. "How about that? My parents haven't stopped smiling."

I smiled at him, and it happened. Just a mild tingle somewhere in my stomach, but enough of a feeling to count: I liked him. And not just as a friend, not just the good-buddy kind of liking. I mean, I *liked* him.

We didn't have much of a chance for private conversation after that; everyone was excited about being at The Sou'wester, and as we ate our BLT's and drank our Cokes, we kept seeing kids we knew. Soon our booth was the center of a crowd, and everyone started getting slightly rowdy. Captain Bill, the owner, looked over once, grimaced, made a thumbs-down motion, and we quieted. It wouldn't do to alienate Captain Bill the very first night; we needed The Sou'wester.

We all walked home together. Everyone lives on or near Shore Road. We made plans to meet at the club beach bright and early. Someone mentioned having a beach party tomorrow night. We sang our old songs, walking along in the moonlight. I knew everyone was feeling just as great as I was.

Except Amy.

"I've got to get some more tan," she wailed. "You guys already have so much from today, and I'm still ghastly white. I feel like a walking ghost."

"No comment, Casper," John said, but the moonlight gave him away. He was gazing at Amy, his expression loving and wistful. As usual, I felt sorry for him. Poor John. More than that, poor Sandi.

John isn't really that cute, and because contacts don't work for him he is doomed to wear those thick glasses, but he does have a nice smile and a good personality. And as Sandi says, he is superintelligent. He's not even eighteen yet and already he's a sophomore at Harvard. More than intelligent, I guess — a genius. Now he was talking about school.

"I decided to switch from political science to pure science," he said. "A drastic change midstream, but I think it's more important to devote my life to improving the physical health of the world. And my very first research project will be . . ."

He dragged out the rest of his sentence.

20

". . . to discover a cure for knobby knees."

I got it only after a second's delay, gave a mock scream of outrage, and rapped him in the arm.

Ross said, very quietly, "I think Nina beat you to it, John. Didn't you notice? *I* did."

I almost died. I think everyone else did, too. There was a sudden, dense silence as we all tried to digest the new Ross. I was secretly very pleased. My legs have improved after years of being bony and much too skinny. Until this year I was worried about them, but now I think they're really my best feature. They're long and slim but nicely shaped, like Mom's and Nicole's.

I couldn't resist flirting.

"You're not going to call me Nee anymore, Ross? Or Knobby?"

I don't know how he managed it so quickly, but there he was, walking right beside me, whispering in my ear.

"I'm just going to *call* you. Okay with you?"

"Okay," I said out loud, because I was so surprised.

"Okay, what?" Nosy Sandi on the other side of me. "What's okay, Neens, or are you just talking to yourself again?"

She is terrible. I gave her the elbow, and she changed the subject.

"Isn't it great to be through with Miss Lowell's for another year? I hope you're not planning to be an artoholic this summer, Nina. You are going to lay off for a while, aren't you? Goof off, enjoy yourself?"

Now she used her elbow — hint, hint.

I smiled at Ross. "Listen to her. What she can't understand is that my art is my pleasure, my work, and my joy. . . ."

I'd made my voice very theatrical, hoping to make him laugh. In a way, I guess I wanted the old Ross back. He was really making me kind of nervous.

"An artist never rests," I continued. "The world is my studio, my life is my canvas."

He was smiling gently, but Sandi made an awful sound.

"Oh, shut up," she said. "I hate dedicated types. Well, that's not for me. I plan to lie in the sun all summer and do absolutely nothing. I'm not going to open a book, not even the juiciest novel. My brain needs a vacation."

"Your brain is always on vacation, Sandi," Amy said, and giggled. The trouble with Amy, though, is she can't make anything sound like teasing. I'm sure she just meant to be funny, but then she made it worse. "Seriously, though, you're never going to get into Wellesley with your marks, Sandi. What I don't understand is that you don't even seem worried about it."

Sandi shrugged. "I'm not worried, Amy — who said I wanted Wellesley?"

I know Sandi can be hurt, even though she never shows it to anyone except me. Amy's marks may be better than Sandi's, but sometimes I think she could used a crash course in simple kindness.

We all try to like Amy. I mean, we've all been together for lots of summers and all our

22

parents are good friends, here and at home. We try to be tolerant but sometimes, when she is sarcastic or cruel, we feel like burying her in the sand.

She doesn't look like she could have a mean bone in her body. Amy is so pretty; I think she's one of the prettiest girls I know. She has the kind of blond good looks that cause people of all ages to look at her and sigh. She's tiny, just a smidge past five feet tall, and she has the kind of confident grace that comes from taking ballet since she was three. If her thoughts and her personality matched her face, we'd probably appreciate her more. Of course, she bothers Sandi more than she does me, but that's because Amy's not my rival.

Except, I noticed now, she was really working on Ross. She looked straight at him and tossed her silvery blond hair. Her hair, always beautiful, looked even better with the moon shining on it.

"Let's go sailing tomorrow," she said. "Good idea, Ross? I don't know about you, but I get so restless just lying in the sun all day."

Not just Ross, but everyone, answered her — a loud chorus: "Good idea, Amy."

She looked surprised and then pouted. She recovered quickly, though. She tucked her arm in Ross's and cuddled close to him. It didn't seem to concern her that he was walking beside me, very obviously beside me.

"So we'll going sailing tomorrow, Ross? What time?"

As small as she is, I decided Amy Sears had a great big nerve.

Sandi was whispering in my ear. "Shall we drown her now or later?"

I laughed. "Now," I said.

"Now what, Nina?" Amy's ears aren't small either.

"*Now* I'm going home," I said. "Good night, all."

Sandi came with me as I knew she would, but everyone else, including Ross, waved and smiled and said good night and "See you at the beach tomorrow."

"Verrry interesting," Sandi commented as we settled ourselves in rocking chairs on my porch. "All these years. Up until this summer we've all been just one big happy family — brothers and sisters, maybe. This summer . . ." She sniffed loudly. "This summer I smell something else in the air."

She lifted her nose and sniffed again. She was grinning. "And I don't think it's mud flats, I don't think it's fish, and it's definitely not roses."

I gave her a look. "What then?"

Suddenly she looked sad. "I was going to be cute and say I smelled a rat. An Amy-rat. I saw her trying to scoop up Ross tonight and at the same time she dropped a few crumbs for John. Except . . . I don't suppose she even knows how greedy she is, do you? That's just Amy — she needs every boy to fall in love with her. I hoped, but I don't know if I'll ever have a chance with John. I thought this might be the summer he'd see the light, see *me*." She sounded so wistful.

"Nee," she went on, "did you ever notice John's eyes when he takes off his glasses? They're so blue blue and soft . . . really nice." There was such longing in her voice. I didn't have the heart to discourage her, but I had seen the way John looked at Amy all evening. Still, I hated to see her so sad.

"He switched his major at college, maybe he'll switch his love life around, too," I said.

She looked at me, and I caught the light of new hope in her eyes.

"Do you think — "

I interrupted her before she said something too hopeful.

"Go easy, Sandi," I said. "The whole summer is ahead and who knows what can happen? I know how much you care about John, and I'd love it if he got smart this summer and . . ." I reached over and patted her hand. "I know you're having heart trouble, but don't listen to Amy. You have a wonderful brain and if you feel like letting it take a vacation, do that. Relax, and things might just take care of themselves."

She didn't smile. "He'll probably never look at me the way he looked at Amy tonight."

Sandi had noticed. I should have realized that; she never misses anything.

"You're my best friend, Nina, and I guess I shouldn't admit this because you might take it the wrong way, but sometimes I'm as jealous of you as I am of Amy. You're so pretty, too,

25

and even Bunny is great-looking this year. You're all so darned good-looking, and *blond*, and I'm so . . ."

She really tried to laugh; Sandi always turned the joke on herself. "Well, anyway, my brother doesn't call me Crow and Cricket for nothing. I'm so skinny and my hair is so brown and *nothing*. I keep hoping I'll suddenly develop this great figure and I try — you know I try — to put on some weight. I practically OD on bananas and bread."

"At least you don't have wrinkles," I said, trying to cheer her up. I had never known Sandi to be so . . . so heartsick.

She didn't laugh. "No wrinkles — yet. Listen, I'm serious. That's the trouble, too — I'm never serious. Good kid Sandi, slightly cuckoo, slightly lazy, and only very slightly decent-looking. I guess I really can't blame John for preferring Amy."

Teasing her, trying to jolly her out of it wasn't going to work. It was important, though, to do some first aid on her ego.

"First of all, you have a model's figure. Even Amy said that, remember? She's too short to be a model. And your hair is brown and beautiful; there is nothing, absolutely nothing, that says you have to be blond to have more fun. That's just a myth put out by Clairol or L'Oréal or something. And you have a talent, Sandi — how about your tennis? You're practically a champion."

She didn't look pleased. "So what."

"Don't worry so much about Amy. You

heard her this afternoon. Remember, she said, 'This summer I intend to meet someone much more mature than what the club has to offer, someone really *deep*.' "

"Mmmm, sure," Sandi said, beginning to smile. "Deep like the hole in her head. She really has to be crazy not to like John."

"Right," I said, grateful that she was coming out of her own deep hole of despair. "Hey, Sandi, did you really look at Ross tonight? Isn't he — "

"He's a hunk," she said. "And he likes you, Neens — a lot. Didn't you get a letter from him this winter?"

I shook my head. "You know it was just a valentine, a joke."

"No joke now," Sandi said. "He likes you. Do you realize that this could be the summer of your life? We're supposed to have a 'summer of our lives,' aren't we? I mean, it's included, isn't it?"

Now she was laughing, back to normal.

"Oh, yes," I said. "It's expected. By sixteen, every American girl, by Constitutional right, must fall in love. Or else."

"So go to it," she said. "I notice Amy had her cute little clutches on Ross tonight. Don't let her get him, too."

I shrugged. "I'm not sure it really matters," I said. "Ross *is* different, but . . ." I didn't want to talk anymore about that. "Anyway, Sandi, just go on being yourself; you do have lots of good points, you know. You're forgetting your sexy tennis elbow. Amy doesn't even know how to play tennis. And you're also forgetting that John plays tennis every morning before he comes to the beach."

"You're great, know that, Neens?" Sandi said softly. "My friend. You always make me feel better about myself."

I stood up, stretched, and yawned. "I'm glad, friend. You do the same for me. But do you think we can go to bed now and continue this discussion in the morning? All this salt air is making me very sleepy."

"Me, too," she said, getting up from the rocker and walking down the porch steps. "Don't you love it, Neens? Being down, I mean. I love Grantham, no matter what happens."

She waved and started across the lawn toward her house. She turned and walked backwards for a few minutes. I waited. "I hope I can dream about John tonight," she said. "Maybe I'll take chemistry or physics or biology — be a scientist, too. Together John and I will discover a cure for . . . well, for something, and then he'll realize what a good team we are, how much he needs me."

It was dark but I knew she was smiling. "Sweet dreams then, San," I said. "And I think you two would make a very good team."

I locked the front door and climbed the stairs to my room. I hoped Sandi would have the "summer of her life." And already it did seem like a different kind of summer. In one day, the boy on the wharf and Ross. Maybe *I* was different. All the summers before, boys hadn't been too important to me. My days had been

28

full and fun: sun, art, beach, movies, sailing. Now? I figured I would just wait and see. Tomorrow.

But it was strange. After I got undressed, got into bed, and put out the light, I cuddled under my blanket and tried to think about Ross. I tried to remember the way he'd looked tonight, the ways he had changed, the things he said to me. But it wouldn't work. No matter how hard I tried to think about Ross, another face kept crowding him out of my mind. This face was indistinct, a face I hadn't really seen yet. It was more of an impression: dark hair, flashing white teeth.

As I felt myself drifting off to sleep, it seemed that the face suddenly loomed very close, the features clear. He was so . . . maybe I . . .

That was all I could manage. I fell asleep in the middle of a thought. I always sleep like a log in the summer. Dad says he does, too; it's the sound of the surf, the ocean's lullaby.

Chapter
Three

In the morning, before the fog burns off, and the sun takes over for the day, Grantham has a special scent, a perfume. I recognize some of the ingredients: fresh white paint, salty air, the roses that seem to climb on every wall and fence, bacon frying. There are other smells I can't identify; maybe you really do have to live on the Cape your whole life to know what they are.

Mom and Dad were still sleeping when I left the house. In an hour or so I would meet the kids at the club beach, but in the summer, early mornings were for me alone. I *like* being alone. Today I had another reason.

When I was little I used to tell Mom that I was going to the cove to "watch the sun wake up." She would smile and nod understandingly and let me go without breakfast.

The day was already beautiful and I could

tell that by noon it was going to be hot. Good, I would make more progress on my tan.

I had on my new white bikini, and over it the biggest, baggiest sweatshirt I could find. Dad is resigned to my stealing his sweatshirts, and Mom confided that now she bought extras — a few for him and a few for me to steal. The big drawstring bag Mom made for me held all my necessities: a small sketchbook, charcoal, fixative, tanning oil, lipstick, my brush, and — making it heavy — the fat new issue of *Seventeen*.

I headed straight for Pate's Cove, and I tried to tell myself that even if I didn't see him again, it was going to be a wonderful feeling to be in my own place again, just the first morning of many more wonderful mornings.

Anyway, I thought, one good, long, up-close look at him, and I'll probably be cured. Just as well probably; I would be free to concentrate on my drawings.

The cove was deserted as usual, and except for the sound of the water breaking gently on the shore, it was quiet, the way I liked it. Even the gulls were peaceful, so I knew he wasn't around to throw them breakfast, or whatever he had dumped from the barrel.

I walked close to the water for a while, my bare toes squishing in the gray satin sand. Then I moved to drier, warmer sand and sat on an overturned rowboat. It was still a bit cool, so I drew my legs up under my sweatshirt and then hugged my knees, making a perfect shelf for my chin. I sat like that for a long time, thinking how much I loved it there, how happy I was to be starting another summer. Most of all, how lucky I was.

The sun was really "waking up" now, rising above the horizon, touching my face and shoulders, warm and welcoming. Then, out of the corner of my eye, I saw a flash of red, and I turned my head quickly.

The bright flash was the sun reflecting on the roof of Pate's Fish Shack on the wharf.

And there he was.

He wasn't barechested as he had been yesterday. Today he wore a short-sleeved T-shirt, but there was no mistaking the straight black hair, the set and width of his shoulders, the tall leanness of him. He was standing near some pilings at the very end of the wharf, and he was shading his eyes as he had yesterday. Only now he was gazing out over the water, toward the line where the sun had just climbed out of bed. I still couldn't see his face.

Not until my chest started to ache did I realize that I was holding my breath. All this over somebody you don't even know, I told myself. And he's probably not even worth meeting.

Still, I might never have another chance, and I had promised myself, hadn't I? I unfolded my legs, pulled my stretched-out sweatshirt down as far as it would go, and walked purposefully toward the wharf. I walked in the water, and I gasped at the first contact. My toes were freezing — it was even colder than yesterday, it seemed — but I figured the icy ocean would help my nerves. As I walked, I kept my eyes straight ahead, not looking at him.

Not that I often walk up to strange boys and say: "Hi — I'm Nina Hale, who are you?" But this was Grantham and it was summer. Easier, somehow.

Dad often walks down to Pate's Fish Shack to buy lobster and to gossip with all "the old salts," as he calls them.

"I don't pretend they're my best friends," Dad says, "or that they do anything more than tolerate me. But I take what I can get, because I enjoy them, their hard-earned wisdom and dry humor that gets by on as few words as possible. Once in a while, I think they get a kick out of my stories, too. At least I like to think so."

If Dad could do it, so could I, I thought.

He didn't hear me coming, or if he did, he didn't turn around until I was standing only a few feet behind him.

"Hi," I said. "I bet you're here to watch the sun wake up, too, right?"

I knew as soon as I said it, it sounded kind of too cutesy, maybe even ridiculous. In the early-morning stillness, my voice seemed too loud.

He turned then and looked at me. I looked back. My first impression of him close-up came as a shock. He was easily the best-looking boy I had ever seen in my life, or maybe it was because his features were so definite and clearcut and his eyes so intense. Until now he had been someone in soft focus — not quite real —

but now the focus was sharp and I wasn't prepared for him. I stared and so did he.

We stood like that, looking at each other, and it seemed like we were both frozen in place, like hours were passing. Behind him, though, the sun was still in the same position, at the point where the sky meets the sea, and I knew it couldn't have been more than a second or two.

"Hi there," he said finally, his voice low and smooth. "Where did you come from?"

I half-turned and pointed back toward the cove.

Looking at him again, I saw that he wasn't really that good-looking, or at least not in any perfect-featured way. It's his coloring mostly, I thought; my eyes noted and recorded the colors almost automatically, in the same way I note the colors I see in an object or scene or any subject I'm thinking about painting. His skin was tan, bronzed, his hair glossy dark with just a hint of red. His teeth were very white against the coppery sheen of his skin, and his eyes were a rich chocolate brown.

The jut of his nose, the slant of his high cheekbones, and his deeply clefted chin reminded me of the photos I had seen of Mayans in a *National Geographic*. I liked his face a lot; I thought of the word my art teacher, Miss Russell, uses: character. Yes, the face had that, and more.

His dark eyes narrowed a little and his mouth curved — a sneer or a smile; I wasn't sure which.

"I didn't think summer girls ever got up this early," he said.

That got to me.

"What makes you think that?" I asked. "Is there a special rule for summer girls? Anyway, what makes you think I am one?"

No matter how much I admired the way he looked, maybe I wouldn't like him at all.

But he just smiled, his mouth soft and peaceful, and I could tell he wasn't upset. I saw the way he was looking at me as if he, too, were cataloging the color of my hair and eyes, the shape of my nose.

I relaxed a little. He leaned back against the pilings at the very end of the wharf and crossed his arms. For the first time he smiled, really smiled. Yes, I decided, he is great-looking and maybe he'll be nice, too, after all.

"My name is Ben Turner," he said. "And please, don't get mad at me. I really have no idea what summer girls do with their time."

I heard that unmistakable accent. If I was a summer girl, he was a townie, or rather, as they're called, a Capie. But I wouldn't say that to him.

"Nina Hale," I said. "We live over on Seaview Road." I looked at him and practically dared him with my eyes. "In the summer only. But I've been coming to Grantham for the summer for as long as I can remember. My dad did, too. His parents had the house when he was a little boy."

Somehow it seemed important that I establish the fact that I was not just some silly newcomer or that I had no claim at all to Grantham. I did. I really felt I did.

"Have *you* lived in Grantham very long?" I asked. Even if he was a Capie, it didn't mean that he couldn't have moved here from another Cape town. Maybe *he* was the newcomer.

It was the wrong question. He scowled. "I was born here," he said shortly. "And I've lived here all my life."

His eyes narrowed as he looked at me. Then I saw his face relax. "I'm out on the boat most of the time. I don't spend much time hanging around town, so I guess our paths wouldn't cross much."

He sounded almost rude.

"Not necessarily," I said. "We buy all our fish here at the shack, lobsters, too. And usually every morning I'm over there." I pointed toward the cove. "Early — when it's quiet, I set up my easel and paint. Or else I sit on the dune there, or on that old rowboat, and sketch. *Every* morning."

He was looking at me blankly as if he had suddenly discovered he was talking to a creature from Uranus.

"Easel?"

"I'm an artist," I said, and turned away. Good-looking or not, I wasn't sure if I liked him — again, I couldn't tell if his mouth was sneering or smiling. I had the feeling, if I said one more word, or he did, we'd be arguing. He had this strange effect on me. I was all jittery inside, emotional. I had never felt this way before because of a boy.

36

"So anyway," I said over my shoulder as I began to walk away, "I saw you from the cove and I just thought I'd walk over and say hi. Sorry if I bothered you."

Why should I bother with *him?* At least Ross Bradford knew how to talk to a girl. And Ross knew what an easel was, for heaven's sake.

He stood up straight and jerked his head in the direction of the shack. "Hey, come on. I have some time before I have to get to work. I'll make you a cup of coffee."

I stopped walking. "You work here?"

"Ayuh, I'm a fisherman. That's what I meant when I said I'm out on the water most of the time. Get up pretty early" — he smiled — "I'd bet even before *you* do, and we go way out. By the time we pull in, I'm usually beat, don't feel much like partying. It's a good life, though — I'm not complaining."

I followed him toward the shack. He opened the screen door for me and stood back, waiting for me to go in first. Hmmm, I thought, his manners were improving. No harm in giving him another chance.

"A fisherman — sounds like fun."

He made a little face. "Hard work, Nina, but ayuh, I guess you could say fun. Nothing I'd rather do."

The interior of the shack was dim and damp, and while I waited for my eyes to adjust to the change of light, I told him, "My dad and Pate Tucker are good friends." I looked at him sideways. "Or at least I know Dad likes to come down here and visit. Maybe you know my father — Whitney Hale?"

Ben shrugged. "Could be. I'd probably know him if I saw him. I've been working for Pate for a long time."

The expression on his face told me the truth, though, exactly how Dad had put it. Pate and the other fishermen and my father were not good friends. Dad was tolerated. And maybe that's what Ben was doing with me. I hated the thought.

Yet beneath his sometimes abrupt manner, there was something about him that reached beyond his words. He was sending me messages with every look he gave. The way he moved, slightly skittish, strutting a little, said: "I like you. Stay awhile and talk to me. Don't run away, Nina."

I guess — I know — I was doing the same thing with him. There was something like electricity zinging back and forth between us, something invisible but very strong. I realized finally what was happening. We were very attracted to each other. It was frightening and wonderful at the same time.

What I didn't tell Ben is that I hate coffee, the taste and the smell of it. It makes me gag. Besides that, inside Pate's shack, amid the barrels and bins and open sinks, something was definitely fishy. Not that I don't like fish, but it was just too much, too early in the morning. I didn't say a word, though, as I watched him measure coffee and water. I kept a smile on my face and tried not to breathe too deeply.

"Where is everyone?" I asked.

"Out there," he said, jerking his head in the direction of the ocean, which we could see through the window over the sink.

"Oh," I said, and nodded, then stopped in the middle of a nod. "How come you're not? Do you have a day off?"

His face clouded, his dark brows knit together.

"I'm needed at home. I guess you could say I'm on call. Anyway, there's lots to be done here."

He took two mugs from a shelf over the automatic coffee machine, and then he poured the steaming brew into the mugs right up to the brim. Then he poured some out of one mug. "Too full, you probably want milk and sugar, right?" He glanced up at me and caught me wrinkling my nose and stretching my mouth into a grimace. He burst out laughing. "Why didn't you say so, Nina? Looks like you're not a big coffee lover. How about some juice instead? I've got some in the refrigerator — cold, not too old. Want some?"

I was relieved, grateful. "Please. Thanks."

"You're welcome." He took a sip of his coffee after he'd handed me a glass of juice. "Was that you yesterday?" he asked.

I took another long sip to cover my embarrassment. He had seen me looking at him. And it also meant *he* had been looking at *me*. I nodded. "What were you dumping out of those barrels? Whatever it was, the seagulls were thrilled."

"Fish heads mostly," he said, and then abruptly, "How old are you, Nina?"

"I'm sixteen." Did I sound defensive? "How old are you?"

"Older than that. I'll be nineteen on Halloween."

All I said was, "Oh," and then, "Where will you be going in the fall? What college, I mean?"

It was a standard question, something you always asked when you met someone that age.

"I've been to school already," he mumbled.

"Oh, well . . . sure," I said quickly. "You don't have to go to college; you already have a profession, right?"

He gave me that squinty look again. "Ayuh."

Ben turned slightly away from me toward the window. The sun streaming in surrounded him, outlined him in gold. Tall, his dark hair haloed with sunshine, his skin red-golden — did he know how beautiful he was? I knew he would hate me to use that word about him; he would be embarrassed. But he *was* a beautiful-looking person.

He turned back to face me, and with his cup in his hand, he settled back against the old sink and looked at me.

"You busy tonight?" he asked casually.

I tried to make my voice sound just right, casual and as offhand as his question.

"I thought you'd never ask."

Was I busy tonight? Hadn't we decided on a

beach party? The first one of the season, which would make it the most important one. And wasn't Ross supposed to call me? It didn't matter.

"What time do you want me to pick you up?"

I hesitated. Maybe I should ask Ben to the beach party. It would be fun to show up with this handsome new boy — show up and show him off. Sandi would go into shock. Amy would be bright green with envy.

No, I thought. Bad idea. At least for now. Later, after I got to know him better.

I handed Ben my empty glass and told him, "Eight-thirty would be fine. Do you know where I live?" He nodded.

Our fingers touched as he took the glass from me, and if I thought there was electricity before, it was small stuff compared to the current of feeling that raced through me now.

He felt it, too, I know he did. His face had a stunned look, and just before he turned to place my glass on the drainboard I saw him draw in a quick, shaky breath.

I picked up my beach bag. "Great, Ben — see you at eight-thirty. Thanks for the juice."

He nodded solemnly. "Ayuh."

I liked the way he said that; I'd never heard anyone say "ayuh" just like that. In fact, what was there *not* to like about him? He was so different from anyone I'd ever known.

As I walked to the sandy stretch that would take me back to the cove, I thought of the conversation I'd had with Sandi the night before.

"Every girl has to fall in love by sixteen," I had said, and she said: "We're supposed to have the summer of our lives . . ."

Well, maybe I was going to. With Ben.

Chapter Four

I left the shack about nine, so when I headed toward the club beach, I didn't really expect to see any of the kids yet. It was much too early for them.

It was so nice walking along the deserted beach, the cold, morning sea lapping at my ankles, a slight breeze rippling through my hair, the sun warm enough now to make me want to take off the sweatshirt.

I thought about Ben Turner every step of the way. Like a favorite record, I played and replayed our meeting, listening carefully to every word he said. He had to like me or he wouldn't have asked me out right away. Or at all.

When I turned the bend and looked ahead of me, I was surprised to see everyone at the beach already; they were spread out on blankets, faceup, like so many frying eggs: Sandi,

John, Amy, and Ross. Even Bunny had managed to get out of bed early.

"Wake up, lazy people," I said as I reached them. "Why aren't you in the water? It's beautiful."

Sandi's eyes opened and closed.

"You're blocking my sun," she said. "And you're crazy if you think *I'm* going swimming. I stuck a toe in before — it's freezing."

I laughed. "Oh, once you get used to it, it's fine."

Ross sat up and patted the blanket beside him. "You *are* crazy," he said, smiling. "Sit down here with us normal cowards."

I hesitated for a second, but I sat, taking care not to sit too close. I didn't want to encourage him, not now.

Amy didn't bother opening her eyes. "Hi, Nina. Did the early bird catch the worm today?"

Had Amy seen me talking to Ben? Had she been spying on me?

Thank heavens, no.

"Stopped by your house on my way down. Your mom said you were already out, probably down at the cove. What's so interesting about that dinky little beach anyway?"

You'd be surprised, I wanted to say, but I didn't.

Sandi snorted. "Nina is an artist, Amy, so that explains everything."

She raised her hand, and with one finger made a circular "She's nuts" motion by her head. Sandi kept her eyes closed, but she was grinning.

Ross was looking at me as I applied oil to my shoulders.

"Did you do any sketching this morning?" he asked.

"No, not really," I murmured. "Just looking . . ."

Amy sat up abruptly and rummaged through her straw bag. She pulled out a brown plastic bottle of suntan oil and handed it to Ross.

"Would you mind doing my back? I can't reach."

She gave him her under-the-lashes, irresistible smile.

Dependable Amy. We could count on her every time. She couldn't stand it if any boy paid attention to any girl, not if *she* was on the scene.

Ross obeyed, but his words were still for me.

"We decided definitely to have the beach party tonight. I've already squared away the fire permit with Mr. Anderson. Good idea, Nina?"

I didn't look at him. I pretended to be very busy spreading oil on my legs. Why was he asking *me*? He said he was going to call me, maybe this was what he was going to tell me about. Maybe he was asking me to be his date.

"Good idea — sure," I said casually. "Summer can't really get started until you start bugging Mr. Anderson. Remember the time you talked him into setting up the tent for us for

45

our Roman beach party? And then you raided your mother's linen closet and brought sheets for everyone to wear as togas?"

"Mr. Anderson's really a good guy," Ross said seriously.

He had changed. But then his old self surfaced.

"Hey, John," he said, reaching over and swiping John's back with Amy's oil. "Look alive. What do you say we take Nina's suggestion and hit the water? It can't be *that* cold."

John sat up and hung his head.

"I was hoping you wouldn't ask. Hey, Ross, do you realize this is the first year we haven't run right in like maniacs?" Then he gave Ross a sly look. "Are we going in now to impress people, or what?"

Ross was standing up, hands on his hips, grinning.

"Sure we are. I don't know about you, but I think I need to do some pretty heavy impressing."

John got up reluctantly and toed the sand. "Aw, shucks, Bradford, do I have to . . ."

Sandi was looking at John and the expression on her face was pure worship. But I saw — and I know Sandi saw — that John was looking at, who else, Amy.

And Ross was looking at me. "How about it, Nina, want to take the plunge? I promise, if you turn blue, I'll — "

I didn't let him finish; I didn't want any promises. Let Amy have him, I thought. I have Ben.

46

"No thanks," I told him, flipping over on my stomach, forgetting that I had put all the oil on the front of me. "I'm just going to lie here and bake. Maybe if I'm lucky I'll fall asleep. I was up early this morning, remember? This early bird needs some rest."

I didn't want to see his expression. I just closed my eyes and turned my face the other way toward the cove.

"I'll go swimming," Amy said suddenly. "The shock will do me good. I'm getting bored just lying here."

I was shocked. In all the years I've known Amy Sears, I have never known her to do anything more than wade and splash herself carefully. She must really want Ross if she was willing to get her hair wet.

Anyway, I was glad when Ross, John, and Amy went running toward the water. I reached over and poked Sandi in the ribs.

"Roll over here," I whispered. "I've got something to tell you."

Sandi wriggled off her blanket and onto mine, or rather, Ross's blanket.

"What?" she whispered back, instantly interested, her eyes as bright as crystal beads.

Sandi is so satisfying. She always wants to hear every detail if I want to tell every detail; if not, she's patient and tactful.

"Start at the beginning, whatever it is," she said now. "Don't leave anything out."

For sisters, Nicole and I are very close in many ways. But she's six years older, and we've never talked about love or boys except in a general way. So, in a lot of ways, Sandi is my sister as well as my friend. She's just the right age, and I know I can tell her anything and trust her with it.

"I met someone." I kept my voice low, but I looked over to make sure Bunny was far enough away. She was; she was fast asleep.

Sandi moved closer. "Who? Where? Start right from the beginning."

"His name is Ben Turner," I said. I was just about to add that he was a Capie, but she beat me to it.

"Turner? That's a very common name around here, a very Grantham name. Is he a . . . is he year-round?"

I really hadn't wanted to say Capie, and I was glad she hadn't either. It didn't sound nice; it was a label just like summer girl, and I knew I resented being called that.

"Ayuh — he is," I said, and grinned.

She laughed. "How did you meet him?"

I told her from the beginning, starting with seeing him on the wharf yesterday and ending with an hour before in the fish shack.

"He's eighteen, almost nineteen," I added. "And he's beautiful. Wait until you see him."

She had her chin in her hands and she looked thoughtful. "Are you going out with him?"

"Sandi, weren't you listening? He's picking me up at eight-thirty."

Her face looked worried. "Are you sure? I mean, do you think you should?"

I stared at her.

"What do you mean?" I asked slowly. Sandi can be opinionated sometimes, but she's never been a snob. "Why shouldn't I?"

She looked uncertain. "I don't know. Well, I guess what I mean is that you don't know him very well. You don't know him at all."

I looked away from her, and I studied the way the tall beach grass grew in clumps in the dune that shielded us from Shore Road.

"What should I know about him, Sandi?" I asked coolly, keeping my voice low and even. "Should I ask him to fill out an application? Should I tell him to list his qualifications, his family background, and three good reasons why I should lower myself to go out with him?"

I jumped when the sand hit my back. I glared at Sandi. "What did you do that for?"

She was mad. "Because you deserved it, Nina. I didn't mean I thought he's inferior. I thought you knew me better than that." Now she looked more confused than angry. "I just meant that he's a stranger. And I guess I said it because it is kind of strange to think of you going out with someone I don't even know. We've stuck together so much, we've really never given ourselves a chance to meet anyone new."

"Okay," I said. "I know what you mean. And if you want to know the truth, I'm kind of nervous about tonight. I don't feel snobbish about it either, but I do think there is a difference, kind of an invisible line that separates us. He called me a summer girl this morning, so he feels it, too."

A smile from Sandi made everything all right between us.

"It *is* exciting, though. Leave it to you to do it first, break out of our happy little group. You know what you are, Neens? You're a pioneer."

"I thought about asking him to the beach party," I said.

Sandi shook her head. "Uh uh — trouble. Ross would be hurt; he's planning on you. In fact, how are you going to explain to him? It sounded like he was asking you to be his date before. If I were you — "

I stiffened. "He shouldn't plan on me, Sandi. I never said anything." I poked her in the ribs again. "Brush that sand off my back, will you? It's sticking, and it itches."

She rubbed at the sand.

"Ouch," I said. "Brush, don't rub. I think I'm burning already. It's still early but it's so hot. When they come back, want to go swimming?"

"Sure," she said. "I'm game. Nina?"

"What?"

"What if it doesn't work out with Ben? What if you find out you don't really like him? Ross is so nice. You could — "

I shrugged. "I don't care. There's this definite feeling I have about Ben. No, it's more than a feeling . . . oh, I don't know . . . I can't really explain it."

It was true. How could I explain electricity? How could I explain that funny, shaky sensation in my stomach, or that strong pull I'd felt every time Ben's eyes had met mine, almost like a huge wave drawing me back with it out to sea. I had wanted to stay with him all day, but I had also wanted to run away fast — yes, it was almost like the tide. I just couldn't put it all into words for Sandi — not yet.

It wasn't necessary. She was looking dreamy. "It does sound exciting. And maybe I do understand. I can't really explain the way I feel about John sometimes, either."

I couldn't really explain, but I still wanted to talk about Ben.

"It's not just that he's good-looking. In fact, maybe you wouldn't even think he is. I don't know, it's just that he's different somehow. Ben isn't like any boy I've ever met. And Sandi, it's not because he's a . . . that he lives down here all year round, or that he's a fisherman. He's more grown-up maybe, but that's not it either. I think I like the way he holds himself, so proud and capable, and at the same time he has a gentleness about him. Do I sound silly? I really don't know him at all; it's mostly just what I sense about him. All I do know for sure is that I really want to see him again. It's hard not to think of him — I mean, you can tell, can't you, San? I can't stop talking about him!"

Sandi smiled and settled herself on the blanket, then propped her elbows up and put her chin in her hands. "That's okay — I don't mind. Tell me more. Describe him again, then tell me everything he said. Right from the beginning."

I laughed. "You *are* a friend." I liked telling her; it was a good way of living it all over again. I left out that scary, wonderful moment when our fingers touched. That was ours, I decided — mine and Ben's. It was too soon to talk about it.

We went swimming as soon as the others came back. All the time we were in the water, and later, lying on the blanket, I thought about Ben. I was beginning to get a little nervous as the hours passed. *What will I wear? What will I say? What if I really don't like him?*

The only thing I knew for sure was that I had a very good tan at the end of the afternoon. Too good. My shoulders were killing me.

Chapter Five

As soon as I got home from the beach, things started to get complicated. I tucked Ben's face in a back pocket of my mind and went out in the backyard to find Mom and Dad. We had company. Then I saw who it was, and I ran to them, thrilled and happy.

Olivia and Andrew Yates are an internationally famous couple. They're both artists; Andrew is a sculptor, and Olivia is a portrait painter. She's painted a president, royalty, actors; and currently she is most famous for her portraits of other artists. Luckily for me, Dad is their lawyer as well as their friend, and now they're my friends, too.

"I'm so glad to see you two," I said, and hugged them both. I *was* glad. They're wonderful, warmhearted, and fascinating people.

"How long can you stay?" I asked, hoping against hope they weren't just down for one night. If so, I would have to reach Ben somehow and cancel our date. Olivia and Andrew are important to me, and not just because it's Olivia who set up my art studies in Paris for next summer. I'll be living with her friends while I attend the very same school she did when she was my age. I had so many things to ask them. I gave a deep sigh of relief when Andrew said, "I think you're stuck with us for a few days, Nina. It's just what we needed, some sea air, and maybe a bit of sea*food* as well."

Naturally they both wanted to know if I had done any sketching that morning. "Your mother tells me you're still at it, waking up with the sun, and going off to your cove-studio," Olivia said, smiling at me. "Well, darling, what inspired you today?"

I almost wanted to say, "Ben Turner inspired me this morning." It was true. I could even tell her about his rich coloring, the interesting slants and hollows of his face, and I could mention to Andrew that Ben's mouth could have been modeled by the finest sculptor. But of course I didn't, couldn't, say any of that.

"Actually . . ." I knew I probably looked sheepish. "I did have my pad and charcoal with me, but I just — "

"Decided to work on your suntan instead."

I looked at Olivia and wondered if she was disappointed in me, but she was smiling still.

Andrew saved me. "Leave Nina alone," he said. "Let her have one day to do nothing but bask in the sun, rest, enjoy, do nothing of any consequence. Which is what we're going to do, Liv. All of the above. We deserve it, it's been a very busy year. Did I tell you, Whit, that Olivia and I ran into your friend, Ken Parson, when we were in London? He's looking very fit, I thought . . ."

I sat with them and listened, and almost forgot that I was still in my bathing suit, with sand down my back, and that my shoulders were very sore. Mom poured me a glass of iced tea, and when she handed it to me, she said: "Don't rush, dear, but as soon as you finish with your tea, I suggest you run up and shower and dress. We're taking Andrew and Olivia to The Colony for dinner, and before that I promised Edith Sears we'd stop by for a drink."

I swallowed hard. Now what was I going to do?

"Wear something nice, Nina — you know The Colony."

I did, of course. The restaurant is set up on a hill just beyond the lighthouse, a huge old Victorian house with lots of porches and more windows that I could ever count. It's a beautiful place, very expensive, and the most formal place in all Grantham. Men are required to wear jacket and tie, women dresses. I finished my tea, excused myself, and went in the house. Mom followed me upstairs.

"Um, what time do you think we'll be getting home, Mom?" I asked, trying to sound casual. Ben would be here to pick me up at eighty-thirty, and I realized I had no way of getting in touch with him.

Mom wasn't looking at me. She stood in

the doorway of my bedroom with her eyes closed, her hand up to her forehead — her thinking position.

"Oh, Nina — I almost forgot. Ross called. He said he . . . wait, let me get it right . . . he said, tell Nina I'll be there around eight-fifteen or eight-thirty to pick her up for the beach party."

She smiled at me. "That's why we decided to have an early dinner, so you can get home in time for the beach party. Your father won't mind running you home if we're not ready to leave. But this way, you'll have a chance to visit some more with Andrew and Olivia, and naturally they understand about your other plans."

She reached over and tickled me under the chin.

"I don't blame you, honey. Ross looks wonderful this year. He's certainly grown up, hasn't he?"

"Yes," I agreed. "But, Mom . . ."

Now she was rubbing cream on my shoulders.

"Too much sun, Nina. You look sore."

I winced and pulled away. "A little, I guess. I should have put my sweatshirt on. Mom?"

"Olivia has a surprise for you," she said. "But I'll let her tell you about it."

I know she expected me to get all curious and try to pump it out of her, but my mind was on something else. I was trying to imagine eight-thirty. Ben and Ross arriving at the same time.

Besides, I was really annoyed at Ross. He was taking a lot for granted. I hadn't protested when he said he was going to call me, but I hadn't said I was going with him tonight. In fact, he hadn't really asked me, had he? He shouldn't just assume . . .

"Be ready by five-thirty, Nina," Mom said. "I promised Edith Sears. She's just crazy to meet the Yateses."

I heard Mom but I really didn't hear her. I was seeing Ben, the way he stood with his arms folded, his eyes narrowed, the chocolate brown eyes, so beautiful.

"I thought The Colony would be a good choice — it's so lovely, don't you think, honey? You always liked it best."

I heard her in the distance. "I . . . oh, sure, Mom . . . I do love him best."

I realized what I'd said the same second she did. She whooped with laughter.

"That's called a Freudian slip — your mistake reveals what you really have on your mind, or I should say, *who* you have on your mind."

A dreamy look came into her eyes.

"Ah, romance — nothing quite like it," she said. "And Ross Bradford, of all people. I can't get over how well he turned out."

"Wait a minute, Mom," I said. "It's not . . . *I'm* not . . ."

She moved across my room and smiled. Just before she closed the door she said, "Five-thirty, Nina. And wear something that goes well with your tan and the stars in your eyes."

I stood there, not knowing what to do. I wanted to yell after her, "Those aren't stars in my eyes, they're tears."

Summer is supposed to be relaxed, fun, easy, simple living. I had to figure something out. And quickly.

I knew Mom loved the idea of a romance between Ross and me. Mom is the one with the stars in her eyes. She loves that I'm a good artist, but she wavers sometimes, telling me not to "miss out on all the other good things." "Be well-rounded" and "A complete person is a happy person" are two of her little sayings.

Nicole disagrees. She makes faces or groans when Mom tells me things like that. Or at least she used to when she was around.

"Our mother is not always right, you know," she told me. "The real truth is that anyone who wants to be good at something — excellent, great — has to miss out on a lot of good stuff. For a while, anyway. Great means that you have to concentrate, be single-minded. Mom had talent, too, but she frittered it away. She used it on too many things."

Nicole ticked off Mom's accomplishments, one at a time on her fingers. "Needlepoint, flower arranging, gourmet cooking, ceramics, macramé, decorating — well, you know."

I did. Mom is good at everything she does. She calls them her "knacks."

I tried to argue with Nicole more than once. "But she is talented. And she seems happy with everything."

"Sure," my sister had said. "A good and accomplished woman — I love her to pieces, and I'm grateful that she made our lives so pleasant — but what about *her*? I ask myself what she could have been. There's a choice, you know — that's not always easy."

Nicole was happy now. She and Ted were both social workers working with special children. "We're both good with people — that's our talent."

Since they got married, they don't get down to Grantham much at all. She says they're too busy with "their kids." Nicole is a wonderful person and a wonderful sister. I wish she were here to tell me what to do.

I got out of my soggy bathing suit, but before I went to shower and dress, I slipped on my terrycloth robe, went into the hall, and picked up the phone. I could have gone down and looked up the Bradfords' number in Mom's little address book, but instead I called information.

Ross's mother answered the phone. She was very friendly.

"Oh, hello, dear," she said. "I'm so anxious to see you. You'll have to come over soon."

"That would be nice, Mrs. Bradford," I said politely. "Is Ross there — may I speak to him?"

"Oh, no, dear — he isn't. Mr. Bradford and Ross went for a little sail. I don't expect them until seven or so. Would you like him to call you then?"

"Uh . . . no thanks," I mumbled. "We won't be home. I mean, we're going out to dinner soon."

"Oh, well, I'm sure you'll see him later as planned. Ross is becoming very punctual, I'm happy to say. See you soon, I hope, dear."

As planned. Ross had even told his mother he had "plans" with me. I was beginning to think of him in the old way — he was a brat.

Anyway, Ross was just going to show up, and there wasn't a thing I could do about it. Cute. Eight-thirty was going to be just adorable.

But I couldn't worry about it right then. It was already after five. I couldn't keep the Yateses waiting. And I did want to talk to them some more. They were helping me so much; they didn't deserve my rudeness.

Rushing — showering, doing my hair, choosing something to wear, getting dressed, trying to make the five-thirty deadline — was a big help. I didn't have time to think.

It was just as well. It kept me from being a wreck. I would just have to handle it. Somehow.

Chapter Six

I love Olivia and Andrew. They're both warm and smart and funny. They kept us laughing all through dinner. Then I remembered that my mother had said something about a surprise, so when I had a chance I leaned toward her and asked, "What was the surprise you were telling me about?"

Mom nodded and turned to Olivia. "Why don't you tell her about Tuesday now? She's bursting. I hinted, Olivia — only hinted."

Olivia and Andrew exchanged glances and then both looked at me.

"Nina, I'm wondering," Olivia said, "is Kay Stein still your favorite artist? I remember that you said she was your idol."

I sighed. "Oh, yes. She's wonderful. My art teacher, Gemma Russell, showed us a film about her this year. Her work is exciting, and I love the way she uses color, don't you? I mean, I wouldn't have thought some of those reds would work together, but they do. Her paintings make me feel happy and . . ." I was searching for the right word.

Andrew and Olivia exchanged looks and smiled. "Would you like to meet her, Nina?"

My breath came out in a loud whoosh. "Like it? I'd *love* it."

"She's invited us to lunch on Tuesday. She has a house and studio in Provincetown this year. We thought you'd like to come with us."

I was so happy. I got up from my seat and went around the table and hugged them both. "You're so great to me — both of you. Kay Stein! I can hardly believe it."

We talked for a while longer, and I must have said thank you twenty times, when Mom looked at her watch and announced, "It's after eight, honey." She leaned forward, her eyes shining, and in a confidential but loud whisper, said, "Nina has a date tonight. He's such a nice boy, and of course we've known the family for ages."

I tried to keep my voice low and calm. "Mom, you misunderstood. I don't have a date with Ross Bradford. I do have a date, though, with someone I just met today. He's picking me up at eight-thirty."

Dad's eyebrows traveled up to his hairline — which is quite a long trip because he has a receding hairline.

"And who is this new person, Nina?"

I looked him straight in the eye. You have to do that with Dad. He has a thing about shifty eyes, probably because he meets lots of people

62

with sneaky eyes and criminal pasts. He practices all kinds of law; he says it keeps him on his mental tiptoes.

"His name is Ben Turner. He works for Pate Tucker. Ben is a fisherman, a year-rounder."

Did I sound belligerent? I hoped not.

"Hmmm, Ben Turner. Yes, I know him — at least, I've seen him around." Now Dad's eyes narrowed. "Isn't he kind of old for you, Nina?"

A better question than I thought he'd ask.

"No," I said. "He's only eighteen." I purposely didn't say going on nineteen as I had for Sandi.

"A fisherman." Mom's voice was flat; it wasn't a question at all. "That means he's — "

"Yes, Mom," I said quietly. "He is."

I turned to Dad. "Would you drive me home now? I have to change my clothes and I don't have much time."

If he really disapproved, I didn't hear it in his voice. He smiled at everyone. "Hold tight, folks. I'll be right back."

I said good-bye, trying not to act like I was rushing away. But I wanted to.

Andrew rose from the table, too. "Listen, let's all go. It's cool enough tonight — Whit, will you make a fire for us? Olivia and I always love our fireplace discussions with you and Alicia."

"Lovely idea," Mom said. "We'll have our coffee then, and I just happen to have a nice, rich dessert in the refrigerator."

A good idea, nothing. Horrible. I was going to have a hard enough time handling Ben and

Ross by myself. Now, it would be a three-ring circus with everyone watching.

I waited for Dad to pay the check, and though I tried not to fidget too much, I guess I did. Enough for Olivia to notice.

"You're nervous, darling," she whispered. "This boy must be very special."

I shrugged, trying to look nonchalant. "Oh, it's not that, Olivia. It's just that I hate to be late for anything."

I corrected myself silently. *Anyone.* And then corrected myself again. *Ben.*

Ross was sitting in a rocker on our porch when we pulled into the driveway. When he saw us he stood up and waved, and I pretended not to notice Mom's bewildered expression.

He looked fantastic! He looked so smooth, well-groomed; his blond hair gleamed like a shampoo ad, and his smile could have sold cases of toothpaste.

He walked over to the car to greet us.

"Hi, Nina," he said. "Guess you'll want to change into something beachy and warm. Don't forget warm — remember how cold it gets down there. Take your time, I won't run away."

Then he greeted everyone else, kissed Mom on the cheek, shook hands with Dad and Andrew, and smiled at Olivia. "It's really nice to see you again, Mrs. Yates."

He was perfect with them, not rude, not

shy. Boy, how could anyone change so much in such a short time?

I waited for my parents and the Yateses to go into the house.

Ross grinned. "So? You're not going to change? Maybe you shouldn't. Set a new style — a dress and high heels at a beach party. Why not? You look very nice."

He wiggled his eyebrows and tried to leer. "I like, I like."

What was I going to do?

"Ross, I am going to change my clothes, but . . ."

He stood there smiling at me, so relaxed and happy-looking. He waited for me to finish my sentence. When I hesitated too long, he asked.

"But . . . ? But what, Nina?"

"You see, Ross, I . . ."

Oh no. Please, no — not like this.

A green pickup truck was pulling into our driveway, stopping just inches behind our Buick.

Ben.

I had to tell Ross fast. "You see, Ross, I have a date tonight, which I made before I saw you at the beach today. I just didn't think you had . . . I mean, that you were planning on going with me."

I felt I should say more, but my mouth was as dry as dust.

I had to give Ross a lot of credit, because he said, without hesitating, "Hey, no problem, Nina. I just thought I'd stop over, and if you were ready, walk you down. Actually, I never did ask you out, at least not properly. My fault. So I'll just go now, and I'll do it better next time, okay?"

He gave me a big (and it seemed, sincere) smile, then half-turned and with a quick gesture beckoned to Ben, a sort of all-clear signal. Then Ross gave me another smile and a wave, and turned and walked away down the driveway. Whistling, no less. Points for you, Ross, I thought. No points for me. I was very jittery.

"Is that your new friend?" It was Mom, lurking just behind the screen door, whispering. "What's he waiting for?"

She sounded nervous, too.

Without turning, I hissed at her, "Mom — please."

I heard Andrew's voice, too, low and amused. "The young fellow is probably waiting for you to stop spying on him, Alicia. Come away now, let Nina handle him. Perhaps he's the shy type."

I could have kissed Andrew. But he was wrong. I was the one who was shy now. Tongue-tied, in fact. All I could do was stand there and wait for Ben to decide to get out of his truck. What was he waiting for?

I finally moved. I walked toward him, making my mouth stretch into what I hoped was a welcoming smile.

"Hi, Ben. Come and wait on the porch while I change my clothes. We just got back from dinner, but I won't take long, I promise."

His eyes had a soft I-like-you gleam, but his

lips were pressed together and he seemed angry or something, but then he shrugged and opened the truck door and got out. He stood there looking at me, his arms hanging awkwardly at his sides.

"I saw you all dressed up," he said. "And *him*. What do you do — have two dates in one night?"

I laughed, relieved. "Oh, Ben — no. I went out to dinner with my parents and our friends, the Yateses. That was just Ross. I've known him for years and years, since we were babies. He just stopped by to see if we were coming to the beach party, and — "

He didn't let me finish. "Beach party? I wasn't thinking of a beach party."

He said it scornfully as if a beach party was silly or childish. Although I hated myself for thinking it, I knew if I somehow convinced him to come to the party, he would stand out like a sore thumb. He wore the same faded old blue jeans and a shirt that was definitely not my crowd's style. He had rolled up the short sleeves, maybe to show off his muscles. His dark hair was combed back, and I could still see the marks, wet and slick. Next to my friends — next to *me* — he looked very different.

But handsome. Looking at him, I had the feeling I had that morning. What he wore didn't matter.

"Oh, we don't have to go to the beach party," I said. "Not if you don't want to."

"Right," he said. "I don't. I've got other plans."

He was looking me over. His eyes were meltingly soft. "You look good," he said. "Don't change."

I stared at him. A dress on a date in Grantham? You just didn't wear a dress unless it was a dance at the club, or for dinner with your parents at The Colony. A dress and heels? Not right.

"Oh, I think I want to," I said. "I'll only take a few minutes."

"I'd like to take you someplace," he said, "to meet some of my friends. We'll dance. A dress is good."

I understood then. He liked the way I looked and would be proud of me. And maybe the girls he knew did wear dresses on a date. Maybe it would be insulting not to.

I was still doubtful, though. "Well, if you really think so . . ."

Had I heard him emphasize *my friends*? He didn't seem to want to meet my friends, but it was all right for me to try to get along with his.

"Come on," he said. "Let's go."

I looked at him. "Wait a minute, Ben. I want to introduce you to my parents. They won't like it very much if I don't. They expect to meet you. So come in the house for a minute, meet them, I'll grab a sweater, and we'll go."

His eyes turned darker, and he looked worried. I patted his shoulder. He seemed nervous and shy again.

"Don't worry," I said. "They don't bite. They're really nice. Plus my dad said he thought he already knew you. He's seen you at Pate's, I guess."

"Ayuh," Ben said, squaring his shoulders and sticking out his chin again as if he were getting ready to march in to battle.

For something to say, and to relax him more than anything else, I pointed to my shoulders, which were bare and very red in my sundress.

"Like my tan?" I asked, smiling.

"Burn," he said. "You look like a lobster right out of the pot."

"A lobster, huh? Thanks a lot."

Now he smiled a slow, sweet smile, and that electric current zinged back and forth between us.

"A good-looking lobster," he amended.

"That's better," I said softly, returning his intense stare. "Much better."

And it was. As soon as I got Ben through the trauma of meeting my parents and the Yateses, we could leave. The worst would be over, and he would relax and be himself and everything would be all right. More than all right, I thought. *Wonderful.*

Ben was wonderful. And no matter what my friends would think of him, *I* thought he looked fine. In fact, I loved the way he looked, so clean and tanned and ruggedly handsome.

"Come on, Ben," I said. "Let's get this over with. I can't wait" — I gave him an under-the-lashes Amy look — "to meet your friends."

Chapter Seven

Ben's bronzed face turned a very red-bronze when I introduced him first to Mom and Dad, then to Andrew and Olivia. I thought they all were very pleasant and easy with him, but Ben seemed terrified. He shook hands with Dad and Andrew and he nodded several times at Mom and Olivia, but he didn't say anything until Dad mentioned Pate's. "I don't think Grantham would be Grantham without Pate Tucker. Not to me, anyway. I'm sure I've seen you for quite a few years, too, Ben. How long have you been fishing?"

He put his hands in his pockets and then took them out again. Ben wasn't quite meeting Dad's eyes and I had a fleeting thought that he almost looked shifty, as if he had something to hide. But no, he managed an answer.

"I was about nine when Dad started taking me out with him, teaching me. Then when I was twelve, I started working for Pate . . ."

His voice trailed off. Dad didn't look disturbed, though. "I imagine you'd like to have your own boat someday, maybe even a fleet? Does that appeal to you, Ben?"

"Ayuh, I might like that. I don't mind working for Pate, though. Things are pretty good the way they are."

Dad nodded agreeably. "Well, there's no doubt in my mind that it's a healthy line of work, and I can't say I wouldn't like it — sometimes I dream about spending my days out there, away from ringing telephones and courthouses. Probably gets pretty cold in the winter, though."

"We just love fish, Ben." That was Mom, smiling too hard, and I almost laughed. What a thing to say! Was it a case of "love fish, approve of Ben"? Not Mom, I could tell.

But I had to feel sorry for her. And she had tried. I could understand; what else could she say? Ben looked so uncomfortable.

"One second," I said. "I'll just get my sweater and then we can go. We're supposed to meet some of Ben's friends and I think we probably should go along now."

It only did take me a second, because I grabbed the first one I could find from the hall closet. Ben looked at me, and I was sure I read gratitude in his eyes.

He seemed to relax the minute we drove away from my house. He smiled at me and asked me about where I'd gone to dinner. Then he just drove, fast and sure, with the kind of confidence that comes from knowing every inch and turn of the road.

"Where are we going, Ben?" I glanced over at him. "You said we were meeting your friends — where do you all usually go?"

In profile he looked even more like an Indian, I thought, the high-bridged nose, the prominent cheekbones, the glossy dark hair.

"You'll like them fine. I've known everyone since the first day of school, some before that. All except Perry. Jimbo Perry's new. He used to live up there in Newton. Then his father died, and Jimbo and his ma moved down here when he was ten. I guess he's the only newcomer."

I laughed. "Since he was ten, huh? And he's a newcomer. Hmmm, guess it *is* true. You have to be born here to be . . . to belong. Right, Ben?"

He didn't notice the slight sarcasm in my voice.

"Ayuh," he said pleasantly.

"Take us," I said, not sure if I was more amused than annoyed. "My grandparents bought the house years and years ago, my father spent every summer of his life here, my sister and I, for all our lives, too. But we're still summer people. I'll be that to your friends too, won't I, Ben?"

"Ayuh."

Ben, I decided, was being a clam. If I put aside a penny for every word he'd said since I met him, would I have five dollars? But then he made up for it a little.

72

"Better watch out for Eddie Griffin and George Doane. They're going to like you, too. I'll bet on it."

"Too?" My voice was soft.

He turned to look at me, and I got a full smile, a brief, approving once-over.

"Sure, I like you," he said. "I wouldn't be wasting gas on a girl I didn't like some."

So he liked me *some*. Well, I liked him *lots*. I would have liked to move closer, to touch his hand. But I didn't.

He read my mind, or at least that's what it seemed like. He pulled into the parking lot behind a small white building with a big painted sign that read THE HUTCH, put the truck in gear, and turned off the ignition. Then he reached for my hand and squeezed it.

"Remember what I told you. Watch out for Eddie and George. Jimbo, too. They're all going to come on to you."

His hand was so warm. "They won't," I said softly, and then added, "They couldn't."

He knew what I was feeling, because he squeezed my hand again and looked very happy.

"Good," he said. "Some good."

The Hutch was crowded; music from a juke-box and voices made it noisy, and small lanterns on each table and in the booths made it dimly lit. I stood waiting beside Ben as he scanned the faces around us, wishing he would take my hand again. I didn't see anyone I recognized, and I felt silly standing there in my cream-colored eyelet sundress, off-balance somehow, as if I had just entered a new world.

Then Ben spotted his friends. He draped one arm around my shoulders and guided me to a booth toward the back of the large room.

Now I knew how he had felt at my house when I introduced him to Mom and Dad and Olivia and Andrew. I could feel the heat rise in my face as I felt five sets of eyes appraising me. Three boys, two girls. Ben said my name and rattled off theirs: Ginny, Phyllis, Jimbo, Eddie, George.

I tried hard to sound confident and friendly. "That's not fair, Ben. Five names for me to get straight and they have only one to remember." I laughed and looked around the booth. "Hi, everyone — nice to meet you all."

There was a general nodding of heads and one of the girls smiled slightly, but I felt their reserve, a definitely cool atmosphere of we'll-wait-and-see.

"How's your ma, Ben?" the small dark-haired girl asked as soon as Ben had ordered a Coke for me and a beer for himself. "She's due any day now, right?"

I turned and looked at Ben. Due? His mother? I realized again that I knew almost nothing about Ben Turner.

I touched his shoulder. "Ben, is your mother pregnant?"

He got a funny look on his face and his lips got thin. "Yep, Ma's having another baby — any day, like Ginny said."

That explained why Ben had said he was needed at home.

"Oh, that's nice," I said. "I've always wanted a baby sister or brother. I used to always beg Mom for one." Then I looked at Ginny, hoping I could get her into a conversation. "Mom always said she didn't have time for another baby. And it's true — she has so many interests, things she enjoys doing."

If the atmosphere had been cool before, it was cold now. Everyone seemed to be looking down at the table. Then Ginny broke the silence.

"Ben's ma is pretty busy, too, Nina," she said quietly and not unkindly. "Five kids with a sixth on the way keeps her pretty busy."

"Five?" I whispered.

Now I really understood why Ben was needed at home.

"Are you the oldest or what?" I asked.

"Ayuh."

Sitting so close to him, I both heard and felt him sigh.

"Want to dance, Nina?" he asked, not looking at me. More than before, I felt like a visiting Martian.

"Sure, Ben," I said. "I'd like to."

It was a slow song, a romantic ballad, sort of sad — one I had never heard before — but it seemed perfect. I got up and followed Ben past the booths to a small space in front of the jukebox. I was glad he had asked me to dance. In the booth I had lost touch with him, felt he didn't like me anymore.

Out of the corner of my eye, I saw that Eddie and Ginny were on the dance floor, too, already dancing, and George and Phyllis were headed in our direction. That meant Jimbo sat alone. I had a quick flash: Jimbo, the newcomer — odd man out.

Then I stopped thinking about anyone else. For the space of that one song Ben held me and I forgot about feeling awkward and out of it. The Hutch disappeared; it was just Ben and me, the wail of saxophones, and a sad voice singing about lost love and how she would never be the same again.

I'll never be the same again, I thought. That current of feeling was so strong now; I felt so happy and so sad at the same time, and yet it wasn't that really. Again I realized I couldn't describe how I felt in words.

I knew Ben felt the same way. When the record ended he kept his arms around me, and though his feet stopped moving, his lips stayed pressed against my hair. But then the next record dropped, and when he heard it — loud, fast — he dropped his arms, moved backward, and grinned.

"Uh uh," he said. "Not me. I can't do that stuff."

As he led me back to the booth he whispered in my ear, "We'll wait for another slow one. Okay?"

It was all right with me and I nodded to let him know that.

The rest of the evening was better. Both Ginny and Phyllis were friendlier, more talkative and accepting, as if they had reached an agreement: "Any friend of Ben's can't be too bad."

Every so often George and Eddie gave Ben a few looks that seemed to be a combination of envy and sympathy, as if they were telling him: "Nina's nice but she's not your type, Ben."

But nothing really mattered except sitting close to Ben, and when the right records played, dancing with him. Once when we were dancing, his arms tightened, his lips left my hair, and he kissed the spot on my forehead where my hair parted. His eyes were soft whenever he looked at me, and when we finished a dance and came back to the booth, he held on to my hand. He didn't seem to mind at all that we were the only couple in our booth holding hands.

At one point I noticed a tall, beautiful brunette sitting alone at a nearby table. She had looked over at us once or twice, and I thought that she was paying particular attention to me. She looked familiar somehow, and I tried to think of where I had seen her before.

"Who's that?" I asked Ben finally. "The pretty woman in the lilac blouse?"

He glanced toward the woman; and his eyes darkened and disapproval clamped his mouth together. His voice sounded scornful. "That's Linda Hutchinson, the owner's wife. She's a cook and waitress in the restaurant during the day. Nights she gets all dressed up and pretends she's a customer."

"I suppose you can't blame her for that," I

said slowly, wondering why there was such a note of derision in his voice.

I stole another look at her. She was really beautiful, I thought, elegant, her silky blouse soft against a golden tan. Her simple jewelry — small gold earrings and one bangle bracelet — and her hair, cut in a becoming style, didn't fit my idea of a cook-waitress. She seemed to be just right for The Colony maybe, but not for The Hutch.

Phyllis sounded just as scornful as Ben had. "Will you look at her tonight? Doesn't she look nice?"

George laughed. "All dressed up and no place to go."

Phyllis made an unpleasant sound. "Boy, she really thinks she's something, doesn't she?"

Ginny didn't say anything, just sipped at her Coke and looked thoughtful.

I didn't say anything either, but I wondered. I wondered even more when I saw her husband — the man Ben called Hutch — come over to the woman's table and saw him say something to her. Then he turned abruptly and walked away. Even from where I sat, I could see the tears glittering in Linda Hutchinson's eyes, and she got up, picked up her purse, and left. I wondered until I heard Ben say, "One more dance, Nina, and then we better get going."

I forgot everyone the moment Ben and I were alone in the truck headed toward my house. I thought maybe he would stop at the spot on Shore where there is a place for cars to park and look out over the ocean, but he didn't. He drove me straight home.

He didn't even turn off the motor, and I sat there for a second or two, waiting, wondering if . . .

"Nina?"

"Yes, Ben?"

"Want to go out tomorrow night?"

"Yes," I said simply.

He leaned over and kissed me lightly on the lips, a kiss that was feather-soft and quick. Then he was back in driving position. Feeling rather strange, I opened my door and hopped down from the truck. As I did, I realized that Ben was the first boy who hadn't walked around to open the door for me or walked with me to my front door. I thought of Mom and Dad and hoped they weren't watching; I had a feeling they wouldn't like it very much.

I hesitated after I slammed the truck door.

"Good night, Ben," I said. "I had a wonderful time."

His smile was brief, just a flash in the moonlight. "Ayuh," he said softly. "Me, too."

And then he was gone, the old green truck rumbling out of my driveway. I felt funny inside — mixed-up, maybe. It was true that I'd had a wonderful time; I liked being with Ben. The feelings were real and strong and very new, and there was no doubt in my mind about Ben feeling the same things. I had seen it in his eyes when he looked at me, felt it when he held my hand. It hadn't been completely wonderful, I thought now. I hadn't really fit in with his friends. They acted as if I were . . . well, face it, they considered me a summer girl. There it was, that invisible line that separated summer people and the year-round, lifelong residents of Grantham. Ben had some of that same attitude but because he liked me, it didn't show so much. It was prejudice, plain and simple. No, the evening hadn't been perfect.

Yet I couldn't deny the attraction Ben and I had for each other, that was plain and simple. I still felt confused.

Chapter Eight

I'm the only early bird in my crowd; everyone else sleeps until nine or ten. Bunny often wanders down to the beach around noon. I was glad. I could go down to the cove and do some sketching. I really wanted to, but even more, I wanted Olivia and Andrew to see that I was still serious about wanting to be a good artist. And today was Sunday; I was quite sure Ben wouldn't be working at the shack. I could keep my mind on my work.

I was wrong. Ben was there — I could see him — and as hard as I tried to concentrate on my first sketch, my eyes kept straying over toward the wharf where he stood. The same as yesterday, he was gazing out to sea.

Finally I gave up. I couldn't see the expression on his face, but something about his posture and the tilt of his head made me think he was depressed. Poor Ben, I thought, it couldn't be easy to be the oldest in such a big family.

Probably he had more responsibility than any boy I knew. I had a pang of sympathy for Mrs. Turner, too. Five children, almost six? I couldn't really imagine it.

Ben hadn't spotted me and I was grateful. In a few minutes I would begin again, and this time I would block Ben out of my mind. I would pay attention only to the scene I wanted to capture, the shoreline with the old, over-turned rowboat in the foreground. It would be nice to paint in oils, too; the abandoned boat was without paint now, an interesting silvery gray.

Ten minutes passed, though, and I was still looking toward Ben, watching his every move as he dumped barrels into the water. I decided that the only way I would get any work done was to draw *him*. The idea appealed to me, since the old wharf and the heavy pilings wrapped with thick rope and the sea beyond was a view I had never done before.

Later I could walk over, visit Ben for a few minutes, and show him the sketch. I'd thank him for being my model, and maybe I'd even give him the sketch as a gift. I turned to a clean page in my sketchbook, propped it up against my knees, and allowed myself a fresh stick of charcoal. I'm so tricky, I thought, smiling to myself. This way I get to look at Ben, see Ben, and get some work done, too. Two birds with one stone.

Not knowing he was my model, Ben didn't stand still for the half hour it took me to finish the sketch, but it didn't matter. I could add details that could make him come to life on the page because I could see him so clearly in my mind. I was pleased with the results, and as usual, when I've been really involved with what I'm working on, I had a wonderful up feeling when I was finished. I guess you'd call it a feeling of accomplishment. Anyway, I was in a very good mood.

As I had figured, Ben wasn't in a good mood; he seemed depressed and edgy, and though he smiled when he saw me coming toward him, I had the feeling that he'd rather be alone.

"I'm not staying long," I said right away. "I promised my friend I'd meet her at the beach."

I couldn't read his expression, and he didn't say anything, so I just kept talking. I heard myself spilling words out so fast and furiously, and I wanted to stop but I didn't dare. I didn't know what to think, except I *did* think, Why are you such a clam, Ben Turner?

"I told you I always come to the cove real early every morning to sketch and paint. I do that every summer, and guess what I did today, Ben? I did *you*."

He was smiling. Thank heavens for small favors, I thought.

"Thanks for being such a great model, Ben. Except I wish you wouldn't have moved around so much — it wasn't easy to capture the *real* Ben Turner, you know. Here, see what you think. . . ."

I handed him the sketchbook and flipped the pages until I came to the one I had just done. "Like it?" I asked.

I really wanted him to like the sketch. I wanted him to like the way *I* sketched. It was important to me because that's who I am. If I listed who I am in the right order, it would come out like this: human being, artist, female, daughter, sister, friend. Or something like that. If Ben liked me, he had to know the most important part.

I look at him hard. "What's the matter?" I asked slowly. "You don't like it?

He had that curly lip look again, the scornful look.

"You do this stuff all the time?" he asked. "Every day?" He handed it back to me. And smiled. "S'funny," he said.

The back of my neck felt stiff, and I couldn't smile back at him. "What do you mean, Ben — funny?"

He shrugged. "I don't know. It just seems funny that someone would draw pictures all the time like that. For fun. I don't know anyone else who'd do that, unless they were an artist or something."

I was shocked and bewildered. I stared at him. Then he made it worse.

"I guess I just can't think of you as one of those arty weirdos; you don't look it, anyway."

I had a terrible feeling in the pit of my stomach. "Arty weirdos? What do you mean, Ben?"

He grinned, crossed his arms over his chest, and leaned back against the pilings.

"Ah, there are lots of them down in the summer, especially over in P-town. The few times I've been down there . . . well, they all wear such weirdo clothes and talk about things that don't make sense. Crazy hats and sandals, and the lady artists wear their skirts too long. You can't get any decent food down there, all this vegetarian stuff. Everyone sitting around all the time — maybe they stick to all that painting so they don't have to work at a real job."

He was smiling but I could see that he meant what he was saying. I struggled to keep my voice calm.

"Ben, what makes you think painting is so easy? Artists work very hard, you know. It's hard, because an individual has to discipline himself or herself. For instance, there is no one standing over me, telling me what to do, so I have to be my own supervisor or boss. That's not easy, but I don't think artists are artists because they're avoiding a 'real' job. That's just not fair, Ben."

He shrugged and his smile had faded. "Can they make a living?" he asked. "Can they support a family? Seems to me . . ."

Maybe he saw the look on my face, because he stopped talking. I wanted to be patient. Maybe it wasn't Ben's fault; maybe Provincetown, which is definitely an artist's colony, does seem strange to a non-artist. Someone like Ben who didn't know any artists personally wouldn't understand that like members of any profession they need to talk about their work. Like me. I don't need all my friends to be artists, but it is wonderful to have someone who talks your language sometimes — Andrew and Olivia, and on Tuesday, the great Kay Stein.

"It takes a lot of training, a lot of hard work, to become an artist — a good artist, Ben. Next summer I'm planning to study in Paris. After that, I'll be going to the Rhode Island School of Design, if I'm accepted. And even after that, it will probably be years before I'm really good — outstanding. The main thing is that I love what I do. I can't imagine being anything else. I think I would probably shrivel up and die if I couldn't draw and paint and *learn*." I couldn't help adding, "I think probably all those P-town weirdos feel the same way."

He threw up his arms in surrender, and his grin reappeared. "Okay, Nina, if you say so. I didn't mean to get you mad. Besides, what do I know? What *I* know is that I love what I do, too. Can't imagine doing anything else, either. And it's killing me that I can't be out there on the water right now. Do you think I like being left behind to clean fish, clean the shack, and dole out fish heads to a bunch of crazy seagulls? I get left behind because I'm the youngest, the least experienced, I guess."

I softened when he said that; I knew now why he'd looked so sad and forlorn before.

Then he said, "What time do you want me to pick you up tonight, Nina?"

A few minutes before I would have said, "Forget it," but now I just said, "Oh, about eight-thirty, I guess."

No matter what, I still felt that special something — chemistry, I guess you'd call it.

He nodded and smiled, and I could see that his eyes were their softest shade of brown. He held out one hand.

"May I have the sketch, Nina? Or are you still mad because of what I said about artists? I like it, you know — it's some good."

In Ben's language I knew now that "some" meant "very." I wouldn't hold anything he'd said against him.

"Sure," I said, tearing the sketch out of my pad. "I already sprayed it with fixative so it won't smudge."

"Thanks," he said very softly.

He didn't move, didn't take one step toward me, but at that moment I felt kissed. Maybe it was just the way he looked at me, the extreme softness of his eyes. I knew he cared about me. At that moment he looked at me with something like love shining from his eyes.

Chapter
Nine

When I got to the beach, Sandi wanted to know every detail about my date with Ben. Telling her was hard. We took a walk along the water's edge because I couldn't talk freely with everyone so close together on three blankets. Ross was being friendly to me but not too friendly, and I was grateful. I didn't want to hurt him. If he asked me out I would say no, and it would be embarrassing for both of us. Let Amy have him, I thought, trying to be fair, but to be honest, Amy and Ross as a couple . . . well, the idea didn't appeal to me too much.

"You'll have to meet Ben, Sandi," I said as we walked along, the water rolling in over our feet up to our ankles. "I'll bring you to the shack some morning and introduce you. I really want you to meet him — then you'll really know what I mean when I talk about him."

I bent over and, cupping my hands, scooped up some water to splash on my face. It was high noon and the sun was scorching. Sandi did better than I did; she sat down in the shallow water and then, taking a deep breath, stretched out until she was lying in the water.

"Ahhgg," she said; then, as she got used to the coldness of the water, she changed it to a contented, "Ahhh."

"You're brave, you know that?" I said, smiling down at her.

Then I copied her, and as soon as I could breathe properly I told her, "I'm going out with him again tonight. Sandi, do you think he could be in love with me?"

She lay there with her eyes closed and her arms folded on her chest, and for a long moment she didn't say anything.

"Well, why wouldn't he be in love with you, Neens?

It was a nice thing to say, but she sounded so sad.

"Any new developments, San? With John, I mean? Are you making any progress?"

A wave, stronger and higher than the gentle little ones that had been washing over our bodies, rolled over both of us, slapping us in the face. We sat up at the same time, spluttering. I laughed but Sandi didn't.

"No," she said. "I think it's a lost cause — I'm a lost cause. John loves Amy. John will always love Amy; I don't have a chance."

I felt so guilty. Here I had just spent a half hour talking about myself and my feelings about Ben, and Sandi had listened with interest. What had I done for her?

"Listen, Sandi. Here I've been wearing out your ear talking about the way I feel about Ben. I don't know if it's going to work out. I told you that he doesn't really understand about me. Even though he apologized, I know I didn't really convince him about my artwork. And he looked at me like he didn't believe me when I mentioned I was going to Paris next summer. No matter how much he likes me, or maybe even thinks he loves me, there's this big difference, you know? I mean, no matter how I hate the idea, hate that he thinks of me and my ways and my family as kind of odd — he does, Sandi. He lives one kind of life and I live another. Can it work? I'm not sure. He is special but, Sandi, how would you like it — being with someone so different from you? At least John doesn't look at you as if you've got two heads. You have something in common with him, even if it's just the fact that you know about and do the same things."

I guess I sounded really upset because Sandi looked at me quickly, peering at me with a mother hen look in her eyes.

"I guess it's true," she said slowly. "We used to look at the town boys and they would look at us, but we never really had anything to say to each other. Isn't that terrible, though — it's really prejudice."

"You've got it," I said. "That's exactly what it is. It's so stupid, too."

"I've been trying to remember what you

told me, Nina," she said seriously. "About just being myself around John. I guess I'm impatient. I want something to happen!" She laughed. "Maybe I should do something outrageous — stand on my head, maybe, or ask him to bury me in the sand. Boy, I guess Mom is right when she says I'm too impatient. Well, I wish I could hurry up and learn some patience."

We both laughed. "See, Sandi? We each like someone — really a lot — but it's still not perfect, is it? Oh, maybe that's not what I mean. There's nothing wrong with Ben. I like the way he looks, the way he is, the way he is with me. But then there are moments when I'm uncomfortable with him. The only thing I do know is the way he makes me feel when I'm with him. I am not imagining that. That's why I want you to meet him. I need your opinion. If the other stuff — his attitude toward me — really shows. If *you* notice it, then . . . ."

Sandi reached over and patted me on the back. "Don't worry so much about it, Nina. Take your own advice and just keep on being Nina. Maybe once he really gets to know you, learns your good points — "

I had to laugh. "Okay, we'll both remember that. We'll both hold on to the thought that we are going to have the summer of our lives. It's only begun, you know. We have weeks and weeks ahead of us."

"You're right," she said. "We're not going to get discouraged, are we?"

I shook my head. I felt better. At least I wasn't totally selfish, monopolizing the conversation with Ben. And Sandi did look happier now and really pretty, with her short, dark curls and deepening tan.

"Still," Sandi said as we approached the blankets and the gang. "He is wonderful, though, isn't he?"

"Yes, he is," I said, meaning it. "No matter what, Ben is wonderful."

Sandi was grinning like a fiend. "I meant John."

Ben was different that night. When he picked me up he seemed cheerful and relaxed. He asked me if I minded "just riding around" instead of going to The Hutch.

"Whatever you want to do, though, Nina," he said. "I just thought it would be nice not to be all tied up with a bunch of people. I figured we could get to know each other better. We didn't talk much last night."

I was happy. There were so many things I wanted to know about him. And there were so many things I wanted him to understand about me.

At first, though, we really didn't talk much, just rode around town and on the pretty, winding road that cuts through the golf course and leads to Tucker's Airport and Brickhouse Pond.

"Got us a couple of Cokes and some potato chips — in case we get hungry," Ben said. "Save us from stopping."

I had a flash. Ben didn't have much money, or at least not enough for a movie date or The Hutch. But even as I thought that, I wondered why he hadn't just told me; it wouldn't have mattered.

When we got to the clearing in the trees that leads down to Brickhouse Pond, Ben stopped the truck, opened the door, and hopped down.

"Come on," he said. "Not too many swimmers here tonight. We can sit on the beach for a while. I'll bring the Cokes."

I agreed, remembering how he had mentioned "wasting gas" the night before.

The pond isn't very big, but it's so beautiful. The water is clear right down to the bottom, and so soft that people come to wash their hair in it. Mom swears Breck or one of the shampoo companies could bottle and sell it as a "natural conditioner." As a change of pace from the ocean, we used to come here all the time, usually in the early evening.

As he had on the wharf, Ben gazed out over the water, with that dreamy expression on his face. I wondered what he was thinking about, so I asked him.

"Oh, I'm just thinking that I'd like to get back out fishing. It's really boring being around the shack all day. But Dad has to go out, bring home the fish, bring home the money. Me, I have to wait for Ma."

He glanced at me quickly. "Not that I'm mad at Ma or anything. I know she's counting on me. The baby could come anytime now, and

I have to be nearby so I can drive her to the hospital in Hyannis. And I'm going to have to move fast when the time comes; Ma has babies one-two-three."

And four-five-six, I added silently. "I'll bet she's glad she has you to depend on, Ben. Tell me about the other kids, will you? Your brothers and sisters — what are their names and how old are they? I only have Nicole and she's married and gone. I don't get to see her very much anymore. It's almost like being an only child now."

"I tease Ma," he said. "She had me first, and then that was it for eight years. It was kind of nice being an only child. No one messing up my stuff, no one else for Ma to fuss over. The boom — the babies started coming. I tell Ma all the time she should have quit while she was ahead, you know?"

He tilted the can of Coke to his lips and took a long swallow. "Billy is ten — he's a real rip. Not bad, but he drives Ma crazy, and me crazy sometimes, too. Sharon is eight, Cindy's seven, and the baby now — not for long — is Andy. He's two. Don't know what Ma will name the new baby. I tell her maybe if she ran out of names, she could stop having the babies to put the names on."

"The kids must really look up to you, Ben," I said.

"I guess they do. They climb all over me every time I come home, always begging me to take them for a ride in the truck." He laughed.

"If I say no to a truck ride, I end up giving them all rides on my back. Ben the Horse."

He was quiet for a long moment, looking straight ahead.

"Ma gets pretty tired. Sometimes I can't go out in the evening until the kids are in bed and the chores are done. There might be times when I can't make it over to your house until later than eight-thirty, Nina. Hope that won't get you mad."

I swallowed hard. It sounded as if he were taking it for granted that we'd be going out a lot, as if I were already his girl.

"I think it's great that you help your parents so much, Ben. Not everyone I know would be so nice about it." I reached over and touched his hand. "Anytime you need any help, ask me. I think I'd enjoy your family." I laughed. "Not that I've had much experience with kids — I never even baby-sat for anyone."

He turned toward me so that his face was very close to mine.

"Nina, maybe it's too soon . . ." He put his arms around me and pulled me close to him. I looked at him, then put my head down on his shoulder.

"That first day when you came up behind me," he said. "I knew then. I knew I would love you. I've never felt this way before."

His lips pressed against my hair, and I could feel them, warm and firm. "I love you, Nina. I know it's quick, but I do. I think about you all the time. Don't go out with anyone else, Nina — just me, please?"

He took one arm away and put that hand under my head and lifted it from his shoulder so that I had to look at him. His face was beautiful in the fading light, his eyes very intense.

"Do you love me, Nina?"

For some reason tears welled in my eyes. I could tell it mattered so much to him. It made me feel humble and grateful and tender. I was frightened, too. Did I want him to love me that much? And did I love him? The way I felt . . . yes, I thought, this must be the way it feels when you love someone.

"Oh, yes, Ben," I whispered. "I do love you. I've never felt this way before, either."

His lips were on mine and we kissed. When the kiss was finished, I put my head back on his shoulder and nestled in his arms. I tried not to think about the questions that seemed to be shouting inside: *Do you really love him? Do you? What's going to happen now?* I had an uncomfortable feeling that by telling Ben I loved him back, I had said much more. In a way, I had answered his request: "Don't go out with anyone else, Nina — just me." And it seemed like Ben was asking that it not be just for the summer, but for always. Had I meant to promise him all that? So soon? I wasn't sure that I could even be the kind of girl Ben wanted. I had so many plans of my own.

But then Ben lifted my chin up and brought his lips down to mine.

"Oh, Nina," he whispered when the kiss ended. "Oh, Nina girl."

I looked up at him and my heart melted. I wasn't going to worry too much. Sandi was right.

Chapter
Ten

We left the pond, but this time when Ben drove me toward home he did stop at the point on Shore Road and parked. We talked some more and kisesed some more, too. I felt so comfortable with him now, not like before when I knew so little about him. Then because it was getting late, I told him I'd better get home.

"I guess you do," he said. "I don't want your folks mad at me. Wouldn't do now."

He kissed me again and then started the truck, and by the light of the dashboard I saw that he was smiling. Not at me, but smiling as if he were happy.

"Walk over in the morning, Nina. Keep me company for a while."

I couldn't help thinking of the sketching I hadn't done.

"I will. Want me to bring you anything? A snack?"

I was thinking ahead, thinking I could get

up even earlier, make some blueberry muffins.

He shook his head. "Don't worry about my stomach," he said. "Just bring you."

He was still smiling when he pulled into my driveway. He put the truck in gear and twisted around so he was facing me.

"Tomorrow night, soon as I can get away, I'll be over. Maybe we'll do some dancing again — at The Hutch — if you want." His smile turned sheepish. "Guess I just want to show off some. Let the guys know you're my girl now."

It was nice to know that Ben was so proud of me. I decided right then that I would bring Ben to our very next beach party; I was proud of him, too.

Mom and Olivia were still up, curled up at either end of our long couch in front of the fireplace. The tail end of a fire glowed and occasionally flickered to a bright flame. It had been slightly chilly and a heavy fog had rolled in, but I knew there would be a fire anyway; a fire was a part of our Grantham nights. They seemed glad to see me.

"Come sit with us for a bit, honey," Mom said. "We've barely had a glimpse of you these past few days. Tell us what's been happening with you."

I could have said Ben is what has been happening to me. But I didn't. I sat with them for a half-hour or so and filled them in on everything. Well, not everything; I skirted around Ben, but I did tell them about his big family and the baby on the way.

Olivia shuddered slightly. "The poor woman — she must be worn to a frazzle."

Olivia and Andrew didn't have any children, so I could understand her reaction, but Mom agreed wholeheartedly.

"You said it. And if Ben is eighteen, his mother must be my age. That can't be easy."

"From what I understand, Mrs. Turner likes having babies," I said.

They both looked at me doubtfully. For some reason I felt I had to defend Ben's family.

"If anyone doesn't have it easy, it's Ben," I said. "His father isn't around much, so Ben is responsible for everything. But he doesn't complain at all. I think it's really great of him."

Olivia gave me a look, partly disapproving, partly loving and amused.

"Sounds like you admire this young man quite a lot. Tell me, darling Nina, what have you been working on? I was hoping you would have some new sketches to show me. Didn't you say you planned to do — "

I interrupted her. "I *did* a sketch today. A study of Pate's wharf. I gave it to Ben. Tomorrow I'll have some to show you, Olivia."

She shook her head vigorously, and her heavy gold earrings banged against her neck. I always love the way she looks, almost gypsyish, with her dark wavy hair piled high on her head, the hoop earrings, the bright embroidered blouses.

"That's fine, darling — just what I hoped. Then you'll have something fresh to show Kay

Stein. I know she'll be interested; I've told her so much about you. Are you looking forward to Tuesday, Nina?"

I smiled at her. "Of course I am. I can't wait."

"Well, then, I thought we'd leave a little before noon. Kay said lunch about one, and then we'll spend the afternoon. We thought we'd have dinner somewhere in town and visit some galleries. Would you like that?"

"It sounds wonderful, Olivia. You've been so good to me."

"That's because I love you, and because I know you have a great future. I want to help in every way I can to further your work."

I sat there with them for a few more minutes, and then I stood up. "G'night, Mom, Olivia. Think I'll go to bed now. I'm planning on getting up really early. Thought I'd make some muffins to bring down to Ben at the shack. Surprise him. Anyway, sweet dreams, you two."

They said good night to me, but as I turned to leave the room, out of the corner of my eye, I saw them exchange frowns. Or I could have been mistaken; maybe their expressions were just an illusion created by the flickering firelight. Anyway, I wasn't going to worry about that. I had other things to think about.

I got up so early that I had to turn on the kitchen light to see to make the muffins. I made cocoa, too, and then, because it was still foggy and really cold, I dressed in jeans and a heavy sweater. I didn't even bother putting on my bathing suit under it; I knew today didn't have a chance of being sunny.

It would be a good day, though, I decided. First I'd visit Ben, then I'd spend some time at the cove and get at least one sketch done to bring with me on Tuesday. Then tonight I had being with Ben to look forward to. And of course tomorrow would be Tuesday — Kay Stein day. This summer was proving to be the best ever. And it had just begun. I had lots of time to be with Ben before I had to go home to Boston and back to school.

Ben was waiting for me, and he was pleased with my breakfast.

"You did worry about my stomach," he said, biting into his third muffin. "Can't say I'm not glad you did."

I stayed with Ben for a long time, but when he began to clean fish, I decided to go find Sandi (and to get some fresh air). No one was at the club or on the beach, so I walked over to Sandi's house. I found her curled up on the windowseat in the living room, reading.

"Aha, I caught you," I said, flopping in a white wicker chair. "I thought you weren't going to open a book this summer."

She looked sheepish.

"Well, I saw John reading it, and I thought — "

"You thought you should read it, too, so you'd have something to discuss with him. Let's see."

She handed me the book and I looked at

the title and then I burst out laughing. "You've got to be kidding! *The Structure of Scientific Revolutions*? What some people won't do for love."

For a minute she glared at me, and then she started laughing. "I made a special trip to the Grantham Public Library for this. You're right, Nina — I'm being ridiculous. I think what I'll do is just ask him if he'd like to play tennis tomorrow. No big deal, just normal tennis. He can always say no, right?"

"Sure he can. Maybe he won't, though. Amy isn't exactly the athletic type, and John would probably welcome a partner who cares more about her serve than her hair."

"Who do you think you're talking to?" she said, her eyes flashing. "In case you haven't noticed, I've been extremely well groomed lately. Look at this."

She closed her eyes and I could see lavender frosting her lids.

"Very nice," I said. "This is the new Sandi Howard?"

"Nope. Just the same old Sandi with a few improvements. Actually, I'm enjoying it. Plus I bought a new tennis outfit, really cute."

"Wear it tomorrow then," I said. "For your match with John."

"I was planning to."

"Wait until he sees you in that, and wait until he sees you in action, Sandi. You'll wow him."

"John's a good player, Nina. Aside from everything else, it should be a challenge. Usually I win, but with John I'm not so sure."

"You're talking about tennis, right?"

She gave me a sharp look. "Yes, but it applies to the other thing, too. I really do think he loves Amy, and that won't change very easily." She grinned. "I'm not giving up, although I think I will bring that book back to the library."

"Good idea," I said. "By the way, will you have time before tennis to walk over with me and meet Ben? I'm just going to stay a short time because I'm going to Provincetown. I won't be around all afternoon and probably part of the evening, too."

"Provincetown? With Ben?"

I shook my head and told her about my luncheon date with Kay Stein. She was very impressed. "I know how much it means to you, Nina. She used to be your idol."

"She still is," I said. "At least, she's the main one."

We made plans to meet on my porch at eight the next morning. She didn't feel like walking on the beach, or downtown, and she thought no one would be at the club. "I think I'll just lounge around for the rest of the day," she said. "Maybe even take a nap. It's a perfect day for that."

But for some reason, I was restless. I wanted to go home and get my sketching stuff, but I didn't. Instead, I headed for the club. For some reason, I didn't feel like being alone, nor did I feel much like sketching. Maybe it was the weather, gray and foggy and damp-cold.

Everyone was in the game room at the club, and they were all happy to see me.

"Sit down, Nina," Bunny said. "We're going to play poker, and Ross had a brilliant idea about what we can use for chips. We've just come back from collecting them."

I had to laugh. In the center of the big round table was a huge pile of seashells. Ross was grinning.

"You *would*," I said. "Leave it to you to think of it — so original."

"At least someone appreciates me," he said. "These clowns complained every step of the way."

And just like that, Ross and I were easy with each other again. He didn't act hurt or mad, and the afternoon went quickly and noisily, with lots of yelling about what should be worth more — quahog or scallop shells, and who was cheating. Bunny was thrilled when she was the big winner, until she realized she was stuck with the pile of shells.

Ross walked me partway home, and to make conversation I told him about Kay Stein.

"That's great, Nina," he said. "What an opportunity. The best thing that can happen to any artist. You'll probably come back very inspired, and then no one will see you — you'll be spending *all* your time at the cove."

I nodded and smiled, but I felt guilty. So far, I hadn't done *any* work, and I had lost my excitement about doing the cove series. Maybe Ross was just saying that about my being at the cove a lot, so he wouldn't have to talk about my seeing Ben so much. But how could he know that? I didn't think Sandi would have said anything.

The time dragged after I got home, and I wished Ben could come over early. I was still restless and kind of irritable. Mom even asked me if I was feeling well. It didn't help at all when Ben didn't show up until nine-thirty.

What did help was going to The Hutch and dancing. His friends were all there and this time they were a little easier to talk to. Being Ben's girl — officially — made me feel as if I had a few things in common with Ginny and Phyllis, although they talked mostly about their jobs and people I don't know. I liked Ginny best. She was pretty, with long dark hair and a soft mouth, and she never seemed to have a bad word to say about anyone. Phyllis was just the opposite. I decided I wouldn't want her as an enemy.

Ben treated me like I was the best thing that had ever happened to him. Maybe I was, although once or twice I saw Ginny look at him, and though she wasn't obvious about it, I sensed she liked Ben a lot. I wondered if he had ever gone out with her. I didn't ask Phyllis, and I decided I wouldn't ask Ben either. If there had been something between them, it was over now. Now it was Ben and me. I hated for the night to end.

It was late and I told Ben I'd better go straight home.

"Whatever you say. I shouldn't leave Ma alone too long either; she's getting real close.

Mrs. Nash — that's Ginny's Ma — she was over tonight. She's going to take care of the kids while Ma's in the hospital. If she's there, I can still see you tomorrow night. What would you like to do?"

"I was just going to tell you, Ben," I said. "I won't be around tomorrow. I'm leaving for P-town at noon, and I probably won't be back until late. I'll stop by in the morning before I go — my best friend, Sandi, is coming with me to meet you. Want me to bring breakfast again?"

"What's in P-town?" he asked, and his voice seemed suddenly toneless and stiff.

I told him. "I'm very excited about it. I can't wait to meet her and see how she works."

He was silent, and it made me slightly nervous. I was remembering what Ross had said.

"It's such an opportunity for me, Ben. I'm hoping she'll really inspire me."

"That stuff really turns you on, huh?" he said slowly. "All that art stuff?"

I tried to laugh to break the awkwardness between us. "Of course. I'm an artist. Or at least I want to be. And not every beginner gets a chance to meet and talk with the great Kay Stein. I'm really lucky. But Wednesday night, can we go out? If your mother's all right, I mean."

"Ayuh," he said, and leaned over and kissed me good night. It wasn't a very long kiss, though, and after I got out of the truck I had barely reached the porch when he was out of the driveway. I stood there with one foot on the first step and wondered about Ben's sudden change of mood. Was he angry just because I couldn't go out with him one night? Or was he upset because I was talking about artists again? I hoped it wasn't that. Anything but that.

Chapter Eleven

The next morning Sandi came with me to meet Ben. She gave me a funny look when she peeked in the bag where I had packed hot-out-of-the-oven cranberry muffins and a thermos of hot chocolate.

"Getting pretty domestic, aren't you, Nina?" she asked. "Since when do you cook so early in the morning? I thought it was your sketching time."

I shrugged and took the bag away from her, and I closed it more tightly to keep out the chilly morning air.

"I enjoy cooking for Ben," I said, and even I could hear the stiffness in my voice. "Listen, Sandi — you'd do the same for John and you know it."

She shook her head no, and then laughed. "Are you crazy, Neens? That would be the quickest way to make him hate me. You've tasted my cooking, remember?"

I nodded and smiled. "I remember. You're right, Sandi."

It was her comment about my using my sketching time for cooking that really bothered me. She was right on target; it was something I'd tried not to think about.

When I introduced her to Ben, she acted just right — friendly and interested — but I noticed how Ben clammed up. He was shy with strangers, or at least with summer people. Not with me, but with my parents, the Yateses, and now with Sandi. After a while, though, things lightened up and I could see him beginning to relax. We were all laughing and having a good time, when the phone rang. Ben went behind the counter to answer it, and it gave Sandi her first opportunity to tell me what she thought of him.

Her voice was low, almost a whisper, but her dark eyes sparkled. I knew before she said anything that she approved. "He's smashing," she said. "And nice, too. I see what you mean, Nina."

When Ben came back from the phone I took one look at him and knew something was wrong. Usually so graceful, he seemed a jangle of arms and legs; he was practically jumping out of his skin. His eyes seemed frantic; they darted from me to the door and to the view of the water from the window.

"I don't know what to do," he said finally. "Ma's ready to go, and Ginny answered the phone when Ma called for Mrs. Nash to come over. They'd just come back from the hospital themselves. Mrs. Nash had a bad fall early this morning — nothing broken but she'll be laid up for a while. Ginny will have to stay home from work and look after her own mother."

He jammed his hands in his jeans pockets, then took them out again.

"I've got to get going. Lock up here and drive Ma to the hospital."

Sandi and I moved toward the door as Ben ran over to the counter and grabbed up a ring of keys. "Fast — I've got to move fast," he said.

I turned at the door. "Ben, who else can you call?" I asked. "Maybe you shouldn't lock up until you call someone. That way they'll have time to get to your house and . . ."

His dark eyes seemed to get darker, black as night.

"There's no one to call. Everyone we know is working. Anyone else is either too sick or too busy. I guess I'll have to leave the kids for a while. I can't take them along — Sharon and Andy are just getting over bad summer colds. Well, maybe they'll be good for a change; I don't expect to be gone too long. I told you, Ma has her babies quick."

I didn't think about it first or maybe I just didn't dare. The words seemed to come out of my mouth of their own accord.

"I'll take care of the kids, Ben. Don't worry. I told you I'm not too experienced, but that won't matter. Your ma needs you now, and I'll be there until you get back."

I thought of Olivia and Andrew, of our plans to leave at noon, and got a funny feeling in my stomach. I tried to make my question casual. "Do you think she'll have the baby before noon?"

He was writing something on a small pad. "Ayuh — don't think it will take long at all. I'll leave a note here for my father. When he comes in for the day, he'll come straight to the hospital and then I can leave Ma and come back for you."

Something clicked in my head and I couldn't look at Sandi.

That meant Ben wouldn't be back until late afternoon.

I could feel Sandi's glare. "Nina," she whispered. "You can't. What about Kay Stein? Maybe you'll never get another chance. What are you going to tell Olivia?"

I had a terrible feeling at the pit of my stomach. I didn't want to think about Kay Stein and her studio in P-town.

"I'm going to call right now," I said firmly. "I'll explain about Ben's mother. And after that, we'd better hurry, Ben. It would be terrble if . . ."

He nodded his head. "Ayuh — I mean, yes, we better get going, but nothing terrible is going to happen. Ma's used to having babies."

I thought then of what Olivia had said about Mrs. Turner probably being worn to a frazzle. I went behind the counter and called my number. Mom answered, and I explained as quickly as I could. She sounded angry.

"Nina, they planned this day especially for

you. Kay Stein doesn't often give luncheons, Olivia told me. She is making an exception, interrupting her work."

Then I was mad. Since when was Mom so interested in my art? Since Ben, I decided. She just doesn't want me liking a Capie. If it was Ross, if I was in love with her good friends' son, she'd be thrilled.

"Well, give them my apologies, Mom. Ben needs me. It's an emergency. They can't leave all those little kids at home alone all day."

Mom sighed. "All right. If you need any help, call me. I suppose Olivia and Andrew will understand your . . . your loyalty."

I hung up before I said anything more. I was angry at Mom, or disappointed or something, because I had a big lump in my throat and my eyes burned. I found my beach bag and picked it up to give to Sandi. I'd ask her to drop it off at my house. I had my new box of pastels with me, and I didn't want anything to happen to them.

But Sandi was gone. Ben was locking the back door, and he walked back toward me and took my arm.

"Let's go," he said. "I already wrote a note, and I've got to lock up the front. Your friend left. She said to tell you she'd see you later."

After that, we didn't talk until we got to Ben's house, a gray saltbox, typically Cape but much smaller than I'd imagined it would be, or should be, to hold such a big family. Mrs. Turner, whitefaced and wincing, was waiting by the front door, a small black suitcase by her feet. She glanced at me and looked imploringly at Ben.

"You think to buy gas, Ben? I'd hate to run out before we get there."

"Don't worry, Ma," Ben said, his face serious and gentle. "We'll make it fine. This is Nina Hale, the girl I was telling you about."

Mrs. Turner tried to smile but she winced instead. "Hello, Nina, glad to meet you." She looked at Ben questioningly. "She riding with us?" She didn't look too happy about that possibility.

Ben shook his head. "Nina's going to stay with the kids."

Ben's mother gave me a doubtful look and gave Ben one, too.

"Did you tell her the water pipe broke? I filled up the tub, though, and some bottles, too. It should be enough to get through the day. Oh . . . oh, Ben — better get going."

Ben helped his mother up into the pickup truck and closed the door after her. He had time for one long look at me. "Good luck," he said. "I appreciate it. I'll be back as soon as I can."

He jumped into the truck, and before I could answer or could ask him anything, he was backing up, turning, roaring out of the driveway. I just stood there, my beach bag in my hand, feeling stupid and not knowing what I was supposed to do next. I hadn't even seen the inside of his house or his brothers and sisters.

To make matters worse, I couldn't remember one of their names, or even their ages. I struggled to remember, and could only come up with one name — Billy, ten: the real rip, Ben had called him — oh, great. I turned toward the house, and as I walked up the path to the front door, I had to stop short. There they were — three faces — peering at me through the front window. They were all smiling at me. No, they were *laughing* — at me. As if I was some strange creature, funny-looking. What had I let myself in for? Whatever it was, I'd better find out, and fast. I could hear something fall inside and break. Then someone crying. It sounded like a zoo.

There were no longer three little faces peering out the front window; I found that out soon enough. One of those faces was in the kitchen, smeared with chocolate batter, standing beside a shattered bowl and the puddly remains of what was to have been a chocolate cake.

"Ma was making me a birthday cake," Cindy explained. "She promised me I could lick the spoon. I'm going to be eight years old tomorrow. Who are you?"

"Nina," I said weakly, surveying the damage. "I'm Ben's friend."

"Ben's *girl*friend," another little girl said. "Cindy didn't mean to break the bowl — it was an accident."

There were all around me, small copies of Ben, dark-eyed and dark-haired, with that same olive skin. The floor was a disaster, pieces of crockery and the brown mixture smeared everywhere. I remembered Mrs. Turner saying there wouldn't be water until later. She *had* said something about filling the tub.

"Come on, kids," I said brightly. "Let me get you cleaned up. Where's the bathroom?"

"Upstairs," Cindy said importantly. "I'll show you."

I would clean up the floor later. I looked at the smallest Turner, the two-year-old gazing at me solemnly from the playpen. I picked him up; he was very heavy.

"Down," he yelled indignantly. "I a big boy."

"Sorry," I said, agreeing. *What was I going to do?*

I found a broom and a dustpan, but I knew the minute I began to sweep up the broken bowl I had made a big mistake. Now the broom was a sticky mess. Still, it was the only thing I could think of, and it didn't help matters that the kids surrounding me thought I was funny.

"Nina made a mess," the girls chorused, giggling. "Ma's going to be mad at her."

Grimly, using a dishtowel, I wiped up the chocolate and threw the towel into the wastebasket along with the messy bowl pieces.

"Ma won't like *that*," Cindy said, her hands on her hips. "You're not supposed to throw towels away, 'specially her best one."

"It's her *best* one?"

Was that my voice? I sounded like I was going to cry.

I left the baby in his pen and followed

Sharon and Cindy and Billy up the stairs to the bathroom. Billy just looked at me scornfully when I asked him if he wanted to wash up.

Using a washcloth, and the tub water as sparingly as I could, I managed to get their faces and hands clean. There was nothing I could do about the stains on their clothes. Now I understood why there had been so much cake batter; with this group, she had to make two cakes. I was a sticky mess myself when I had finished. Good thing I was wearing one of Dad's oldest sweatshirts over my jeans.

When I got downstairs again, Andy, "the baby," was whimpering.

"He wants his diaper changed. And it's time for lunch."

They all stood there in a circle around me, watching my face. Then they pulled out the chairs from the big kitchen table, and pushing each other, almost knocking another dish off the table, they took their places, looking at me expectantly.

"What you going to make us for lunch, Nina?"

Andy was really crying now.

"Want me to get the diaper for Andy?" Sharon asked.

"Yes, please," I said softly. I had never changed a diaper in my life. It took me ages. Andy seemed too big to still be in diapers.

I'd wondered why Mrs. Turner still kept him in the playpen. A moment later, I wasn't wondering. Andy toddled around as soon as I finished, and his chubby little hands were reaching for, and touching, everything in sight. I scooped him up and put him in the high chair.

Lunch next. *Was* it lunch time? I thought of Olivia and Andrew, probably leaving at this very minute for Provincetown and Kay Stein. I didn't have long to dwell on it.

"We want lunch, Nina. We're hungry. Do you love Ben?"

I nodded. "Sure. What do you usually have for lunch, kids?"

Billy, the so-called troublemaker, was quiet, almost dignified, and not so little. Couldn't he have watched his brothers and sisters for one afternoon? No reason, I thought, why he can't at least help me. I looked at him.

"How about *you* making some lunch, Billy? I said, smiling at him. "I'll help you, but you know where things are and . . ."

He gave me an incredulous look and shook his head.

"No way — that's ladies' work. My pop doesn't cook, Ben neither."

I could have killed him, or at least given him a better answer than just a weak, "Ohhh."

"Ma was going to make fish chowder today," Cindy said. "Why don't you, Nina? It's easy."

I went to the refrigerator, hoping against hope there would be chowder, or something, already prepared. Something I could heat up for this mob. I opened the door and stared into the interior — and almost died. There, lying on a platter was a large fish, one eye staring up at me coldly, accusingly. I shut the door. If they thought I was even going to touch that fish, much less clean and cut it up for chowder, they were crazy.

I searched the cupboards and came up with several cans of chicken noodle soup and a box of Saltine crackers.

"Don't like chicken noodle — want vegetable beef," Sharon said.

"You're having chicken noodle," I almost yelled.

"Won't eat it," she said, pouting.

"Then don't," I said grimly, struggling with the can opener.

I got through lunch, another diaper change for Andy, and then settled them all in the living room with the television set on and a pile of toys. I let Billy go out to ride his bike. "Be good, kids," I said firmly. "I'm going to do the dishes."

"No water," Cindy said.

She was right, of course, but I went back to the kitchen anyway, to clean up as best I could. I was glad to be by myself for a while, away from all those dark, watching eyes. And they were quiet, busy and, happy. I sat down at the kitchen table and looked around. Ben's house was cluttered; the furniture was all old and scratched, and the curtains at the window were limp and dingy. There was all kinds of kids' stuff littering every surface. I couldn't help compare it to my own airy, bright, and beautiful summer house, and the even nicer one in Boston. Mrs. Turner — all the Turners, including Ben — didn't have things very easy.

I was glad the kids were being so good. What would I have done after lunch if they depended on me to entertain them? I wandered into the small living room, smiling, thinking for the first time how really cute they all were, how much like Ben — especially the oldest, Billy, and the youngest, Andy.

I stopped short. There, scattered on the floor, were my brand-new pastels, and Sharon and Cindy each had a sheet of my expensive paper, torn from my pad. I saw immediately that almost every piece was broken. They were happy, pleased with themselves.

"Thanks for bringing us crayons," Sharon said, smiling sweetly. "We like to color."

"I can see that," I said, and it wasn't easy saying it from between clenched teeth.

Then I relaxed a little. I could always buy more of them, and they did seem grateful for the bright crayons.

"I like to color, too, kids," I said brightly. "In fact, I'm an artist."

It wasn't exactly a voice I heard, just a loud, definite thought: *Are you, Nina?*

Chapter Twelve

Ben came home about four-thirty. The kids were already making hungry noises again.

"We've got us a cute little sister," Ben told his brothers and sisters. "And Ma's fine, says to give you all a big hug for her."

He did that and then he turned to me. "And one for you, too, Nina — from me. Thanks."

He hugged me and kissed me while everyone giggled and jumped around us. Except Billy, who said, "Yuk," and walked away, out of the room.

Ben laughed and called after him, "You just wait, Billy-boy, till you're my age and you meet someone like Nina here."

I wasn't sure, but I thought I heard another "yuk" from the kitchen.

"How did it go, anyway?" he asked, looking around. "Did you find everything you needed? Ma said she hated to see the cake stuff go to waste, but I told her you love to bake, told her about the muffins you've been bringing me. I figured you just went ahead and finished making the cakes."

I looked at him, saw how sweetly he was smiling at me. For a second or two, I hated him.

"Sorry, Ben," I said shortly. "I couldn't. Cindy knocked the bowl off the table." I glanced over at her; she was scowling at me. "By accident, of course."

"Nina ruined our broom," Cindy said. "And she threw Ma's good dishtowel in the trash."

For such a small girl she had a lot of nastiness in her voice. Should I tell him how they ruined my new pastels? I wondered.

Ben had stopped smiling. I turned away, picking up my beach bag.

"There wasn't any water," I said. "I did my best."

He crossed to where I stood, put his hands on my shoulders, and looked deep into my eyes.

"I know you did, Nina, and I'm obliged."

He said that for everyone to hear, but then he leaned closer and whispered into my ear: "I love you, Nina."

I wanted to say it back, but all I wanted to do was to go home and sleep. I had never realized taking care of kids could be so tiring. How did Mrs. Turner do it?

I guess Ben read my mind. "Okay, kids, I'm

taking you for a ride — go hop in the truck. Billy, go get Andy's car seat. We're all going to take Nina home now."

"I don't think I'll make it out tonight," Ben said as he drove. "I've got to work on that water pipe, and, well, I'm beat. I might even put myself to bed with the kids. You don't mind, do you, Nina?"

I reached over and patted his arm. "I don't mind, Ben. I'm tired, too."

With only little Andy in the front seat between us, I knew I'd be safe in telling him I loved him out loud. I was just about to, when he glanced at me and said, "Probably better that way. Get a good night's sleep so you'll be fresh for the kids tomorrow. I don't know what I'd have done if you hadn't offered to watch them while Ma's in the hospital."

I stared at him silently. What *had* I offered? This morning I thought he understood that it was just for one afternoon, while he drove his mother to the hospital. Then I remembered that I had offered to help him out with the kids that night at Brickhouse Pond. What had I gotten myself into? I had looked forward to one of my usual mornings at the cove. I had planned to even skip my visit with Ben. I had to get some sketching done.

"I'll pick you up early," he said, and then he grinned. "Crack of dawn. Ayuh, I'll be happy to get out on the boat again with my father. I missed it some awful."

He was going out fishing and leaving me

with four kids all day. *What had I gotten my-self into?*

"How long . . . I mean, will your mother be in the hospital very long?"

He shook his head as he maneuvered the turn into my driveway.

"Not long — three, four days. Not long enough, Ma says. She tells us it's her only vaca-tion." He laughed. "Ma can be real funny."

Real funny, I thought glumly, got out of the truck, and waved to the kids sitting happily in the back on blankets and boxes.

Very funny, I thought later, lying in bed; and all during the next three days, I tried to see something funny about being cooped up in the small, messy house with four into-everything kids. I tried, too, to make the kids like me, but Cindy had a grudge against me (because of the bowl, the broom, and the stupid dishtowel) and did everything she could to aggravate me. Cooking, I either made too much of everything or too little. I never knew little kids could be so critical. "Ma doesn't wash dishes that way," or "Ma never makes us brush our teeth before we go to bed, just in the morning."

I couldn't wait for Ben to get home every night, and after that I couldn't wait to get home. I was glad it took until eight-thirty for him to pick me up, and I was so sleepy by ten-thirty I couldn't wait until he took me home again. I loved him, but I was angry at him all the time.

"What's the matter, Nina? You mad at me or something?"

I always denied it, told him I was just tired. Childcare *is* tiring, and I told him so.

"Ayuh, guess it is," he said calmly. "At least till you get used to it. When we get married, how many children do you want?"

I was stunned, even as tired as I was, I sat up straight and stiff in the truck seat. *"When we get married?"* I said with astonishment.

I could only see the flash of his teeth by the dashboard lights.

"Ayuh. Guess I never did ask you proper yet."

"No, you never did."

I couldn't believe he was saying it. I guess it just never occurred to me that *anyone* would ask me to marry him, at least not for a long time.

"Well, now I'm asking proper. You love me, don't you, Nina?"

I did. I *did* love Ben. Just sitting next to him was enough to make me know I cared about him more than any other boy I had ever met. The electricity was as strong as ever, no matter how much I complained to myself about baby-sitting every day.

"Yes, I do," I said softly. "I love you very much, Ben, but . . ."

He sighed. "You'll have to graduate first, I guess. But next June you'll be all finished with school, and then your parents can't object. We can get married right off and then have the whole summer for our honeymoon. I can be looking for a place for us — "

It was hard to talk, hard to think straight.

"Ben — wait a minute. My parents *will* object. I'll only be seventeen when I graduate. And I've planned to go on, study art. I've planned to be an artist for years, Ben. I told you I'll be going to Paris next summer."

I couldn't see his face clearly, but the small noise he made in his throat was the kind he made when he wasn't pleased.

"Seventeen's not too young," he said. "Lots of girls are married and have their first baby by the time they're seventeen, eighteen. Nothing wrong with having your kids while you're young and strong."

I couldn't answer him right away, but I couldn't help thinking, Or old and frazzled like your mother.

"I'll have to think about it," I said carefully. "You took me by surprise."

Then his arms were around me, and for a long moment I couldn't have said anything even if I wanted to. Ben was kissing me. I could feel his love for me pass from his lips to mine. I did love him, and I guess I loved having him love me so much.

It was romantic, I decided. My first proposal. But I was upset, too, and I yearned to talk to Sandi. I realized I hadn't talked to her — or anyone — since the first day I went to Ben's house.

It was another day and a half before I was

free to find Sandi and the gang at the club, and by that time my mother was fit to be tied.

"What is this, Nina?" she asked in a tight voice, closing my bedroom door and leaning on it. "What is all this baby-sitting? Are you planning on taking care of Ben's family all summer? This is not what your father and I had in mind for you, not at all. First you can't keep your engagement with the Yateses and Kay Stein, and now you don't even have time for your friends. Not to mention us, of course." Her normally mild eyes were fiery. "It's quite obvious we are far down on your list of priorities. Then, Nina — last but certainly not least — there is the matter of your art. How long have we been in Grantham, and what do you have to show for it? You wasting all your time on this . . . this local boy . . . and what can possibly come of it? It's not as if you have anything in common, or that the relationship can go anywhere. Of course, Nina . . ."

I stared at her and for a minute I didn't like her at all. I could understand that she was worried about me, that she didn't like to see me missing all the good summer stuff, but saying that about Ben? *Local* boy? Nothing in common? Mom sounded so snobbish.

I stopped listening, although I pretended I was. I had my own thoughts.

Up until now my life had been pretty smooth. Lucky girl, and I knew it. Lots of girls at school had problems, were unhappy, and more than once a few had cried on my shoulder. I always felt sorry for them and tried to help, but their problems were never my problems. I had great parents and a great life. Until now. Now I had something to worry about. What was I going to do about Ben?

That morning, walking to the cove, my beach bag packed with a fresh sketch pad, charcoal, and my old set of pastels, I thought of something else that Ben had said. Rather, something he hadn't said. He had ignored me when I said I planned to go on, to study art in Paris. He didn't take that part seriously, didn't care about it.

Well, I cared. In fact, I cared so much, my fingers were actually itching to hold a stick of charcoal, to feel the smooth whiteness of my pad, to lose myself in drawing. I had missed these early-morning times alone, but I hadn't realized *how much* I missed it. What was I going to do? I loved Ben. I loved my art, too.

Later in the day Sandi reminded me of Mom. Only she said things Mom didn't say.

"You're crazy, Neens. I mean, this is summer, remember? You're supposed to have a good time. And you've even lost your tan. You look terrible, positively unhealthy."

She was right. My tan had turned yellow. All those days spent mostly in the house. The sun was bright today, the water a sparkling jade frosted with whitecaps. I had missed this, too.

"Don't yell at me," I said, trying to smile. "It isn't my fault, and it isn't Ben's either. He — they just needed me to help out for a while."

"Good. It's great to be needed, but come on, Nina. Have some fun now. At least now you'll be able to catch up. For instance, the next beach party is tonight. You're coming, Nina." She jabbed me lightly on the shoulder. "With Ben or without him. Come tonight. We miss you — I miss you. I've missed talking to you."

I wanted to hug her. I'd felt the same way about her. Instead I splashed her with water and she screamed. "Don't get my hair wet!"

I burst out laughing. "Oh, no, not you, Sandi." I looked at her more closely. "You do look great. How are things going with John?"

She looked peaceful. "So-so. We're playing tennis every morning, and now when he's looking for someone to swim with or take a walk on the beach with when Amy says, 'No, thanks,' I say, 'Yes, thanks.' We're talking more. At least he's getting to know me — the real Sandi Howard."

She paused, and then went on. "Actually, Nina, nothing dramatic is happening. We're just friends, same as always. Still, we have fun together, and I think he's surprised that we have so much in common. And we laugh at the same things. That's important, isn't it, Nina?"

I nodded. "It sure is. It sounds good, Sandi. It sounds as if you're really making progress."

Sandi couldn't have known how much what she'd just said would bother me. Sandi and John — so much in common. And Mom's "It's not as if you have anything in common with . . . that local boy."

I felt like crying. Sandi was suddenly standing closer to me, peering into my face.

"Nina, what is it? What's the matter?"

At that moment I was so grateful for her.

"It's just that I'm confused," I said. "Ben is . . . Sandi, he asked me to marry him. And he doesn't understand about — "

Her eyes flashed angrily. "He doesn't understand about anything. Does he even know who you are? He keeps you away from us, and worse than that, away from what you really like to do. Nina, have you done anything you planned yet? You're letting it all go for him, aren't you?"

I nodded, fighting tears.

"I love him, Sandi — I really do. You met him, you know why I love him so much."

Her voice was thoughtful. "Yes, I met him, but I don't *know* him. Nina, I think it's time to show him who *you* are, how you live. All you ever do is live *his* life, go with *his* friends. Come to the party tonight and bring Ben. Maybe seeing you in your own setting will help him to know you better. And, asking you to marry him? Doesn't he know how old you are? Didn't you explain about Paris next summer?"

"Yes, I did. But he doesn't seem to want to hear it. Ben thinks seventeen is a fine age to be married. He says lots of girls down here are married with babies at that age."

I could see by her expression what she thought about that.

We talked some more, and I decided I would

ask Ben to take me to the beach party tonight; Sandi was right. It was time he did something I wanted to do. When he came over to get me tonight, I would tell him, not ask him.

When I got that settled in my mind, I forgot all about Ben — or almost — for the rest of the day. I had a wonderful time. I could feel my skin soaking up the sun's rays. I was so happy to be on the beach, I kept running in the water, making everyone else come with me — in general, acting like someone just out of prison, or something. Ross was sweet to me, but Amy stuck pretty close to him, and I didn't get much chance to talk to him. A couple of times he looked at me and smiled, and though I still didn't want to encourage him, I smiled back.

"How's your new boyfriend, Nina?" Amy said once, as she clung to Ross's arm. "He's from around here, isn't he? Is he nice?"

Her tiny, perfect nose was lifted haughtily, as if she couldn't believe anyone local could be nice.

"He's wonderful," I said. "You can see for yourself tonight. I'm bringing him to the party."

"Oh, goody," she said, showing her tiny, perfect teeth. "I can't wait to see your mystery man."

I made a face. "Ben is not a mystery man, Amy."

She tossed her head and looked up at Ross, twin dimples appearing in her cheeks. "Oh, but he is — you've sure been hiding him from us."

I decided not to argue with her, and besides, I didn't want to talk about Ben with Ross standing there.

Later, I thought about Amy's calling Ben a mystery man. In a way she was right. I didn't really understand Ben. More than that, I knew he didn't understand me. Maybe tonight would help change that.

Chapter
Thirteen

At the far end of the ribbon of sand that is our club beach, we are allowed to have a fire for our parties. Someone, long before our crowd discovered the fun of beach parties, had outlined a circle with large rocks. We were held responsible for making sure the bonfire was out at the end of the night. Tonight the fire was extra big, extra beautiful.

Ben hadn't wanted to go. "I've never been to a beach party, never wanted to, and I don't now."

I wouldn't take no for an answer. "You'll love it, Ben," I said, and it was more of a command than persuasion. "Besides, I want you to meet *my* friends."

I guess he got the hint, because he shrugged and said, "Okay, Nina, I'll go."

"Great," I said. "But I'm going to run back in the house and get you one of Dad's sweatshirts. You'll freeze, even with the fire."

I was thinking of his comfort, really, but also of my own. He had one of those terrible black T-shirts, the kind with the pocket, and, as usual, he had rolled up the short sleeves.

As Ben and I headed down the beach, I could hear my friends even if I couldn't see them. I could see the fire ahead, blazing brightly. Ross probably made the fire, I thought. He had always been good at that. I remembered his teasing us about being a Boy Scout. At the time none of us had believed him.

Ben was nervous. "What do you at these things?" he asked, his hand clammy in mine.

"No set thing," I told him. "Sometimes just talk, or sing the old songs, play games, munch, tease each other, be silly. It's never the same thing. Guess it's just fun being off by ourselves, and the beach, the fire . . ."

It was dark, so I couldn't see his face, but I could have sworn he didn't look convinced.

"I love the ocean and hate the beach," he said grouchily. "The sand is already in my shoes."

I laughed, hoping he would cheer up before he met my friends.

"Take 'em off, silly. I did, remember? No one wears shoes on the beach, Ben."

He stopped, and I waited until he took off his shoes and socks.

"Cold," he muttered.

He started to walk again, carrying his shoes, but I put my arm around him. "Wait a sec, Ben. Don't be in a bad mood. I've tried to get along with your friends — don't you think you should try to do the same? You're acting like I'm leading you to the electric chair. Relax."

"Nina . . ."

He let his shoes drop on the sand and then his arms were around me. "I'm sorry. I guess I'm not being a good sport. Do you love me?"

He took me by surprise. "Yes . . . of course I do."

"I love you, Nina. I don't like to share you. Not with my friends, or yours. I want you all to myself."

"That's nice, Ben, but impossible. At least some of the time we should do things with other people. It makes our times alone more special."

He didn't kiss me, but his arms stayed around me and he held me tight for a moment. I was quiet, but I couldn't help wondering why I was being so sensible. A few weeks ago I couldn't have said that about not being alone so much. I wouldn't have wanted to. I had an impulse to break away from him now and hurry toward the fire and the group ahead of us.

"We'll have fun, I promise," I said, and then I did move out of his arms. "Don't forget your shoes or the tide will steal them."

Everyone was there, and they all looked up when I led Ben into the circle around the fire. "Hi, people, this is Ben Turner."

I made the introductions, and this time Ben had the problem of keeping all the names straight.

The only one he knew was Sandi, and thank

heavens for her — she managed to get him into a conversation right away. Amy was staring, and the look in her eyes was pure admiration. I was glad and then mad. Amy had better not move in on Ben tonight, although Amy — being Amy — would try.

I was right.

"How come I've never seen you before, Ben?" she said, crouching beside him, giving him her devastating eyelash look. "If I *had* seen you, I'm sure I wouldn't have forgotten very easily."

She was so obvious, she was so ridiculous, she was so pretty.

Ben liked it.

There was no question about it — Ben was beautiful in the flickering firelight. He looked more like a Mayan prince than ever.

Even Bunny sat up and took notice. "We haven't seen very much of Nina this summer," she said. "I can understand why."

Sandi was sitting beside John, and while she snapped open cans of Pepsi and passed them around, he watched her. He was smiling.

Amy stopped making eyes at Ben and cuddled up to Ross. After a while, Ross draped his arm around Amy's shoulder, but it didn't seem more than a friendly gesture. Then I wondered why I even cared. What mattered was that Ben was sitting close beside me, and I loved him very much.

Amy kept trying to make conversation, and the things she said, the questions she asked, were embarrassing. Maybe more to me than to Ben, because when he answered her he had a slight smile on his face. After a while I didn't know who to be madder at, Amy or Ben. Ross was being Ross, the *old* Ross, and he decided we were all going to play charades.

"The party's too quiet," he said. "Everybody's too comfortable. John, you go first. I had my mother make up some stuff, write them on slips of paper, so I can play, too. Get off your duff, Carlton — look alive."

I was glad Ross had planned something, or else I might have spent the whole evening fuming, trying to keep Ben's eyes on me. But no matter how hard we tried to make him do a charade, Ben wouldn't.

"I've never played and don't know all those signals. Maybe next time."

He didn't even seem embarrassed, just firm.

Ross was funny. He went through all kinds of antics, and I couldn't help but notice how cute he was in a cream-colored Shetland sweater and matching corduroys, which he had rolled up to the knee. His hair looked like burnished gold in the light of the fire. He didn't have much to say to me, directly, but he smiled at me once, very directly.

After charades, Bunny and Sandi produced a huge paper bag and dumped the contents on the blankets. Huge bags of potato chips, Fritos, pretzels, and one superlong bag of popcorn.

John took one look and hooted. "Here we have one of the finest fires in Grantham Yacht

Club history, and we have to eat popcorn from the 7-11. Couldn't we have popped our own? Lazy, lazy people."

I heard Sandi laugh. "Who are you kidding, John? You're the one who went shopping for our munchies."

She sounded so happy and confident, I thought. Not like the Sandi who had been tearful and hopeless at the beginning of the summer. Well, good. Great. I was happy for her.

For a while everyone got up and milled around. Ross and Amy and Sandi took a walk to the water's edge. From where I sat I could see only the silvery phosphorus that frosted the dark ocean, but I could hear it, the breakers strong, noisy. I was surprised to feel a tap on my shoulder. I looked around and so did Ben. It was John, standing there awkwardly, a sheepish smile on his face.

"Excuse me, Ben. Could I borrow Nina for just a few minutes? I want to ask her something. I need some advice."

Ben mumbled something, and I jumped up and walked with John into the darkness.

"Before Sandi comes back," John said in a low voice, "I want to ask you a question. You're her best friend, and I thought maybe . . ."

He hesitated for a long moment, and I felt sorry for him.

"Sure — ask me anything, John. I'll be glad to help if I can."

"Listen, Nina, I like her a lot. Would you have any idea how she feels about me?"

I was so glad it was dark, or else my huge grin would have given it all away. I swallowed twice before I answered to make sure there was no laughter in my voice. I wanted to be honest.

"She likes you, too, John. But what about Amy? All these years . . ."

He made a disgusted sound. "Amy. I never realized how insubstantial she is. Amy doesn't know what she wants, or who she wants. Anyway, I guess I just outgrew her. Sandi . . . well, there's a lot to Sandi. I can talk to her and she's smart. Do you realize what a really great girl she is, Nina?"

"I realize. That's why she's my best friend. My advice, John, is to tell her how you feel. You said you can talk to her so . . . talk to her."

"I'd hate to make a fool of myself," he said, and his voice was mournful in the damp darkness.

"You won't, John," I said, smiling. "One thing I do know, Sandi does not think you're a fool."

He gave me a quick hug. "Thanks, Nina. I guess I just needed a push. I've been wanting to tell her how I feel. I'll tell her tonight."

Lucky Sandi. At least everything is working out for her, I thought as I went back to the fire and Ben.

I caught myself just in time. What did I mean? Things were working out for me, too. We were both having good summers, we were both in love with wonderful guys. Ben was wonderful.

139

As the party went on and everyone settled around the fire, it was even more obvious that Amy thought Ben was wonderful, too.

"Do you ever take anyone out fishing with you, Ben?" she asked in her sweet little voice. "I mean, I think it would be so great to see what real fishing is all about. I never met an authentic fisherman before."

Didn't he see how phony she was?

Either he was putting her on, or he was thoroughly enjoying himself.

It went on and on, and Sandi's sympathetic glances didn't help matters any. I didn't want anyone to feel sorry for me. Amy was being so Amy that it was stupid to be annoyed or jealous, but — I had to admit it — I was both.

I didn't mean to say it.

"When I graduate, Ben and I may get married. I'll live in Grantham all year round."

There was a deep silence, and then Bunny walked over to me and gave me a big hug.

"Oh, congratulations, Nina, the first one to be engaged. It's so romantic."

I could feel Sandi's glare and I didn't want to look at her, but I did, and I was right. She *was* glaring at me, her eyebrows knit together, her eyes shooting sparks.

Ross was looking but he wasn't glaring. He wasn't smiling, either. I felt like a fool.

Ben had pulled me closer to him, and in almost a reflex action, I put my head on his shoulder and closed my eyes. *Why had I said that?*

I was jealous. Not of Amy and her perfect

face and gorgeous blond hair. Ben was the one who worried me. He was so appealing, so agreeable to everything Amy said and did. He didn't know what she was like. He was flattered. Damn him.

I thought of Ginny and wondered again if she cared about Ben, too. I would be a fool not to do everything I could to keep him interested in me, keep him loving me.

But did I really want to marry him? Live in Grantham all year? Mom and Dad and I had spent Thanksgiving in our summer house one year. We had a wonderful time and a wonderful dinner, but we all agreed that Grantham was deadly boring and quiet in winter.

I was quiet on the way back up the beach. Ben had his shoes to carry, so he didn't even try to hold my hand. I was miserable. His voice, loud in the quiet, startled me.

"What was the point, Nina?"

My voice was loud, too. "What do you mean? What was what point?"

"Inviting me along just so I could meet all your boyfriends?"

I was so shocked I couldn't answer right away.

Finally I said, "What are you talking about?"

"That preppy, Ross — glamour boy. And John: 'Could I borrow Nina for a moment?' "

I didn't hear his shoes fall, but suddenly he was gripping my shoulders with both hands. "Did you say that about marrying me just to make them jealous, or what?"

I couldn't help it; I started to laugh. "Oh,

Ben, you've got it all wrong. And I guess I did, too."

Standing there, I told him what I had felt, my anti-Amy feelings, my suspicions about *him*. I felt his hands relax on my shoulders, and then his arms went around me and he was kissing me. Once, twice, and one more long one.

"Sorry," he whispered.

"Sorry," I whispered back.

"Our first argument," he said.

"I love you, Ben."

"Nina?"

"What, Ben?"

"Did you mean it? You'll marry me next summer?"

"I don't know, Ben," I whispered. "Maybe."

He kissed me again, and I decided not to think about anything for now. The moon was white and full, high over our heads. It was a perfect night for being with the person you loved. I was so glad it was Ben. And I was glad summer wasn't over yet.

Chapter Fourteen

Summer was hurrying along faster than I ever remembered. Maybe it was because I wasn't getting up early anymore to go to the cove. Sometimes Ben would take me home early — eleven or so — but when I got home I was usually restless, not able to fall asleep right away. I would toss and turn, think, and that would make me toss and turn even more.

I did go to the club beach every day, but it bothered me to see everyone having such a good time, as if they didn't have a care in the world. It was hard to join in their easy laughter when I was so out of it now. Buying clothes for school in the fall, what colleges we were going to apply to; those subjects didn't hold any interest for me. What did all that matter if I was going to get married right after graduation? What was worse, I couldn't say anything to Mom and Dad. I already knew what their reaction would be. They would be horrified. They would be disappointed. So would Nicole. So would Andrew and Olivia Yates. They would absolutely howl with objections.

But if summer seemed to be flying by because sleeping late made the days shorter, every day I seemed to fall more in love with Ben.

Being with him so much, I learned how patient and sweet he was, how gentle he was with his brothers and sisters, how thoughtful he was with his mother. Mr. Turner didn't seem to be around much; he was either fishing or sleeping. Ben's father was a silent man. If I thought Ben was reluctant with words sometimes — a clam — then Mr. Turner was a stone. He was the father of all those children, but to me it seemed like Ben was. He was the most responsible boy I had ever met. When I thought about being married to him, I knew what a solid, good husband he'd be.

But I didn't like his attitude about money. One evening I asked him if we could stop at some gift shops. It was Nicole's twenty-third birthday at the end of August, and I wanted to get her something really special. Besides, I hadn't even been in one of the many shops or boutiques all summer. Usually it was one of my favorite things to do.

Ben hated it. He tagged after me from counter to counter, to rack or display, and made terrible grunting sounds; his face was screwed up in a constant scowl.

"You thinking of buying something here, Nina?" he asked.

I looked at him and nodded. "If I can find something I like. Or rather, what Nicole would like. So far, I've seen lots of possibilities, but I haven't decided yet."

"You wouldn't catch me buying something here," he said, giving the small shop a scornful once-over. "They ought to be shot for these prices. It's nonsense stuff, anyway. Who'd pay two dollars and fifty cents for a bar of soap?"

I shrugged, but annoyance started to heat my face. I had thought about the soap. For Mom, not Nicole. Mom loves good English soap.

"Look at this," he said, picking up a small wood carving of a seagull. "Ten dollars. Crazy."

I tried to ignore him. We had about four of those same wooden seagulls in our summer house, and a few in our house in Boston, too. They were nice, they reminded us of Grantham through the winter months.

I picked up a soft Shetland sweater, the exact color of raspberries. I loved it. It was my size and I was going to need some new clothes for school. The price was thirty-five dollars. I had more than that with me. I hesitated for a long time, my fingers caressing the soft wool. Then I got mad at myself. My hesitation was because of what I knew Ben would say. Well, he wasn't my husband yet. I could buy anything I wanted. I picked up the sweater and walked with it to a display of silver jewelry. I could feel Ben breathing down my neck.

145

"What have you got the sweater for? You're *not* going to buy that?"

He had this amazed look on his face when he picked up the tag. "Thirty-five dollars? Do you know how much food that would buy?"

"I like this sweater, Ben. Yes, I *am* going to buy it. And this, too."

I held up the silver bracelet for his inspection and showed him the tag. "Nicole collects silver bangles. She has about a dozen of them now."

I retraced my steps back to the soaps. "This, too," I said. "My mother is partial to English Orchard soap."

I knew I was being arrogant but I couldn't help it. He had ruined my shopping trip, made me feel like a spoiled rich girl. Which I knew I wasn't. I didn't require lots of things but I did love *nice* things, and I couldn't see what was wrong with that.

His mouth tightened, and he looked down at the floor. Then he shrugged and looked up at me, his eyes a very dark and hard brown.

"Not for me to say. So long as it's *your* money you're spending."

I nodded slightly, but inwardly I was very aware of what he had said, what he had meant: "When it's my money — when we're married — you won't be spending money for nonsense."

It bothered me for the rest of the day, and for days after that I thought about Ben's attitude. If I married him, would that be the end of pretty sweaters and all the small luxuries I was used to? Maybe, I decided. But I could show him my ways, how things like that could make life more pleasant. I could work it out.

A few nights later, Ben took me to The Hutch.

"Big night," he said as we pulled into the parking lot. "A group's playing instead of the jukebox. Look at all these cars."

The Hutch was crowded, but Ben had asked his friends to get a big booth so there'd be room for us. They were waiting for us, called to us gaily, and it made me feel good to be wanted. Phyllis and Ginny would most likely be my best friends if . . .

"Hi there, Nina," George said, grinning slyly. "Got a good tan, looking good."

Ben gave him a playful swipe with his hand. "Watch it," he said, "No playing up to" — he hesitated, and then he added — "the girl who just might be my future wife."

I nearly died, and I felt heat rush up my neck and into my face. When I could manage it I looked around the table, but there was no surprise on anyone's face, just smiles.

Phyllis leaned toward me. "Just *might* be, Nina? Haven't you said yes yet?"

I resented the cat-curious look on her face, and I also had a sense of unreality, as if marriage to Ben was only a fantasy, something that didn't really have anything to do with me. I wanted to shout: "Leave me alone — I'm only sixteen years old. I'm too young, there's too much I want to do. I'm going to Paris."

But no one would leave the subject alone.

Phyllis and Ginny started telling me about other girls they knew who were already married; most of them hadn't finished high school.

Phyllis went into detail about a friend of hers who was "really lucky" because she and her husband already had a dining room set and some nice living room furniture, and by next year they were going to buy a bedroom set, "better than anyone's around here."

I was fascinated and horrified. I listened to all their talk about furniture and dishes and mothers-in-law, and I just couldn't relate any of it to me.

But I smiled and acted like it was all very interesting and possible that I, too, would be into all that stuff next summer.

"You've got a wonderful guy," Ginny said softly, and again I got that impression that she cared about him a lot. "He'll be a good husband, better than most of them around here. It's good he's letting you finish high school, though. It will come in handy if you have to get a job."

I heard only two words: "letting you." If you were married did your husband have to *let* you do things? It was a new thought, an upsetting thought.

"I just hope you won't be like her," Phyllis said, jerking her head toward the table near us. "That one's a real case."

I looked. Sitting at the table — alone — was the pretty dark-haired woman I had admired that first night, the owner's wife, Linda Hutchinson. She didn't look like a "case" to me. I thought she looked lovely, poised, and beautifully dressed.

"What's wrong with her?" I asked, trying to watch the woman without being obvious about it.

"Oh, she's just weird, that's all," Phyllis said impatiently. "I mean, there's nothing wrong with the summer people, but they should understand that we do things a little different down here."

I looked at her, and I guess she saw how confused I was.

"I just don't think you'll be like Linda because you're more sensible and all. Look how you stepped in when Ben's mother was in the hospital. You don't need all kinds of fancy dates or to go around all dressed up in expensive clothes. Linda . . . well, she was a summer girl, too — kind of rich, too — and her folks had a fit when she married Hutch. It was her choice not to finish school — she told me she was studying at Chamberlain in Boston to be a dress designer. Now all she does is act like she thinks she's some kind of special person, dressing up like she does all the time having her hair done at the beauty parlor twice a week, spending all of Hutch's hard-earned money. Worst thing is, she acts like she's unhappy all the time. She expects Hutch and everyone to treat her like a queen. Do you know what she did?"

Ben saved me from knowing what Linda Hutchinson had done. I didn't want to know. Already I had a big lump in my throat, and I felt like crying for the beautiful woman with the haunted eyes.

I noticed, though, that Ginny hadn't joined in the conversation, and I thought I saw sympathy in her eyes. Again, I thought how much I liked Ginny. She was kind. I knew she could be my friend.

Ben led me to the dance floor and put his arms around me.

"The first slow music," he said. "I've been waiting for my chance."

I had to smile at him, but as I did I felt my lower lip tremble, and I buried my face in the soft flannel of his shirt.

"Are you mad at me, Nina?" he whispered in my ear. "I guess you didn't want me to say anything about getting married yet."

I couldn't answer him. I was afraid to.

"I couldn't help it, I guess. I'm just so proud of you and" — he pulled me closer — "and I love you so darned much. You're the most beautiful girl in the world."

Why did I think then: *I wonder if Hutch told Linda the same thing.*

With Ben holding me, the soft strains of "Color My World" sounding in my ear, I couldn't help loving Ben back.

But I had never felt sadder in my life.

Later, when he drove me home, he wanted to stop and park along Shore Road.

"Not tonight, Ben," I said softly. "Maybe next time. I'm really tired. I don't know why, but I've been very tired lately. I can't keep my eyes open."

He was agreeable, but I couldn't look at him. It was a lie. I knew I wouldn't get to sleep easily at all. There was too much to think about.

Chapter Fifteen

During the next two weeks I invited Ben to my house, once for dinner, and once just to "sit around." Both times he sat there, scrubbed and handsome — and definitely ill-at-ease — and answered "Ayuh" and "No, sir" to Dad's friendly questions. Mom, he called "Ma'am," and I could tell by the look on her face that she hated it. My mother says she *thinks* young and therefore everyone should understand that she *is* young. Ma'am is not the title you give to someone like my mother. But of course Ben didn't know that.

I wanted my parents to like Ben, but how could they? They couldn't pry anything out of him. Most of the time he couldn't even look them in the eye. I knew it was shyness, but I wasn't sure Mom and Dad knew that. At the end of both those evenings I felt hopeless. More confused than ever.

I made an effort to get up early every morning, and I trudged down to the cove, determined to get back to my plans. So far, except for the sketch I had given to Ben, all my efforts were pretty feeble. In other words, bad. I seemed to have lost my touch. Gemma Russell was right about a lot of things, I thought, especially about her insistence that an artist never rests, never stops working to improve. Looking at the awkwardness of my sketches, though, I was sure she was wrong about my being "burdened with talent." The only thing I seemed burdened with this summer was my own mixed-up mind. Did I want to spend my life being Mrs. Ben Turner? Or didn't I? One minute I was sure I could never say yes to him, the next minute — especially when I was with him — I was sure I couldn't say no.

At the beach one afternoon during the last week in August, Sandi practically dragged me into the water.

"It's so hard to talk to you these days, Nina," she said, giving me a disapproving look. "You say you're happy, that you're madly in love with Ben, that you wouldn't have it any other way, but you sure don't *look* happy. You might be able to fool everyone else but I know something's wrong. Is it about Ben wanting you to get married? Haven't you told him you can't yet? You have to, you know."

It was a bright, hot day, and the water sparkled around us. Sandi looked really nice in a hot pink bikini, her dark hair longer than she'd ever worn it, pulled up in twin pony-tails, her tan dark and smooth as molasses. I saw the worry in her eyes.

"I don't know what to tell him, Sandi," I said, and my voice had a funny, ragged edge to it. "I might want to marry him. I mean, I can't stand the thought of losing him, going to Paris next summer, not seeing him during all that time. I thought maybe if I did get married next summer, I could take art lessons from someone good in P-town. I wouldn't have to give it up, you know. I could make Ben understand how important it is to me."

She looked at me with her don't-kid-me look. "Nina, what you're saying is that Ben doesn't understand now. Does he even know or care how serious you are? Most important, how *good* you are? Neens, you're the only girl I know who has had a one-woman show."

I shrugged. "That was only at Miss Lowell's — big show."

"Stop it, Neens. You can't remember how excited you were? How excited everyone was? We're so proud of you, all of us. And did you ever think of how lucky you are to have parents who are willing and able to give you the best education and introduce you to the most helpful people? I know I'm lecturing, but — "

I bent over and played with the water. "Yes, you are," I said. "But it's okay. I guess I needed someone to give me an opinion. I get so mixed up sometimes, trying to decide. I can't hurt Ben. If I say no, he'll —"

I heard Sandi's sigh of exasperation. "Oh,

Nina, stop thinking about how Ben will feel. Think of yourself right now, think of what it will mean for your whole life."

I felt her hand on my arm, and her voice was full of warmth.

"By listening and caring, you helped me with John. I'm having a wonderful summer now. Everything worked out fine. It might not be forever, though. I don't think John will be the only guy in my life. Nina, we both have years ahead of us. Think about it — *years*."

Everything Sandi was saying I had thought myself, so I couldn't be irritated with her. I knew she was just trying to be helpful because she cared about me. Maybe she was right when she said Ben didn't understand how serious I was about wanting to become a fine artist, but I thought maybe that was partly my fault. I had told him about my plans, but had I been living them?

In the beginning of the summer when I first met him, I'd said that I was at the cove every single day, and yet I hadn't been. Of my own choosing, I had gone to Ben's house to stay with his brothers and sisters and given up a day with Kay Stein. I had talked about Paris and art school but I'd said, "Maybe," when he asked me to marry him. Why wouldn't he be confused? I talked art but I didn't live art. And I knew very well from my reading and from Gemma Russell that there are lots of people like that. "Pseudo-artists," she calls them, and says, "They like the thought of themselves as creative individuals, but they hate the work."

She had compared those people with would-be writers. "They love the name Writer, but they can't stand the paperwork." Just a short time ago, I had been just as scornful of that type as she was. Was it Ben't fault?

Sandi let me be silent, didn't push. We left the water and started to walk, shivering a lot, but we didn't go back to the blanket for our towels.

"I guess I will have to decide something," I said. "It's my fault more than Ben's that he doesn't really understand. And you know what? Ben does understand how it is to love something so much. He feels that way about fishing — he talked about it one day. I'll bet if I really tried to explain, make him see —"

"And then what?" Sandi asked quietly. "Even if he knows that you want to continue your studies after you're married, maybe with someone in Provincetown or Boston, do you think you could really do it? Don't you think you'd miss living in Boston? You're the one who drags me to the museums and the galleries. And Paris, Nina — could you seriously consider giving up that chance? It's your *life* you're talking about, your whole life."

"I know that," I said. "Do you mind? Can we stop talking about it for a while? My head needs a rest, I think. I haven't been able to think of anything else."

She smiled and wrinkled her nose: "Sure, no problem. Hey, I just remembered — are you going to the Labor Day Dance at the club?"

I just looked at her. Labor Day? The summer

was almost gone; I couldn't bear the thought. "I'm not sure," I said, and then, "Probably not. I don't think Ben will want to."

She bent down and splashed her face with salt water. "I hope you will, though; it won't be the same without you, Nina. In fact, it really has been kind of a strange summer for all of us. Different from all the summers before."

"The summer of our lives, Sandi?" I said forcing lightness into my voice.

She shrugged. "I doubt it."

I didn't answer, but I would have said the same thing. Because right now I had lots of doubts. Too many.

Chapter Sixteen

Nicole and Ted were due to arrive any minute. They hadn't been down all summer, and Mom insisted they at least take time out for her birthday. Mom was excited, fussing with food and flower arrangements. Dad, not I, was sent to buy a dozen live lobsters at Pate's Fish Shack.

I wrapped Nicole's present in the prettiest paper and ribbon I could find, and placed it with the other packages on the coffee table in the living room. I was anxious to see my sister, but Mom would probably fill her in about Ben and me, and then, I knew, Nicole would lecture me, too.

I didn't think she'd have the same attitude as Mom, but I knew she thought it was important to "give up the good stuff in order to be great at what you do." She always talked about concentration, single-mindedness.

Nicole was twenty-one when she married Ted, but I had to admit that she'd already graduated from Wellesley, and now both she and Ted were working for their master's degree in social work. No, I didn't think she would understand or approve of my marrying Ben next summer.

Earlier, I had asked Ben to have dinner with us. "My sister and her husband are coming down. Would you like to have dinner with us and meet them? You like lobster, don't you?"

He had looked at me, then shook his head slowly. "I'm not much good around your folks, Nina. I guess we just don't talk the same language. Maybe I'll see you later if you can get away."

I'd thought about asking Ben to the Labor Day Dance, too, but I decided not to. The dance was a dress-up affair: Girls wore dresses; boys, dinner jackets. There was always a sit-down dinner, a good band, flowers on every table — an elegant finale to the season. It wouldn't be fair to ask him; I knew without asking that Ben didn't own a dinner jacket, and I didn't think he'd want to go out and buy one.

Ben had an invitation for me, though. "You're invited to my house Monday night. You're the guest of honor, Nina. Ma wants to give you a good dinner for watching the kids when she was in the hospital. Up until now, she's been too busy."

I was touched. "She doesn't have to do that, Ben. I was glad to help."

Now that it was behind me, I could say that. And I did like Mrs. Turner.

"Wear that white dress," he said. "The one you wore the first night we went out, okay?"

"Okay," I said. I thought of my friends, pictured them at the club Monday night, but I would be all dressed up, too. I would spend the last night of "the season" with Ben and his family. The thought shouldn't have bothered me if I really loved him, but it did. I have to admit it really did.

Now, waiting for Nicole and Ted, I tried to push away all those thoughts, but all I could think of was that no matter what, I still had the same feeling for Ben every time I was with him. The attraction, that electric feeling, hadn't weakened one bit. If anything it had grown even stronger, despite all the doubts and questions in my mind.

Then I heard Nicole's voice and I raced out on the porch to greet her. She shrieked and I shrieked even louder, and we hugged and clutched each other until Ted pulled us apart. "Me, too," he said, kissing me, his face wreathed in a rosy smile, "How's my favorite sister-in-law?"

"Your *only* sister-in-law is fine, thank you," I said, realizing as I did how glad I was to see them.

An hour later we were all in ecstasy eating our lobster, laughing at each other as the drawn butter dribbled down our chins. Mom had made a huge tossed salad and toasted some French bread; there was lots of white wine, and there was still a pile of bright red lobsters awaiting us on a huge white platter.

"Heaven," Nicole said, groaning with pleasure. "Absolute, unadulterated heaven."

"Well, it's about time you two had a taste of lobster and Grantham, which I agree is heaven," Mom said happily. "You two work so hard. You don't have any summer at all."

Nicole was working on the tiny lobster legs, the part that no one else bothers with. "Ah, that's so true, Mom — *this* summer." She was smiling. "But *next* summer . . ." I saw her glance over at Ted, saw him give her a nod. "Next summer Ted and I are going to Europe. We've been saving every spare penny and plan on two whole months." Now she looked straight at me. "We'll be in London, Germany, Switzerland — and then, at some point, we plan to visit our famous artist sister in Paris. We wouldn't think of not seeing Nina or Paris."

Nicole and Ted were both looking at me now, smiling expectantly.

"Well, Nina?" she said. "How about that? By that time you'll be familiar with everything and you can be our tour guide."

"It's *great*," I said. "We'll have such a good time, too." I smiled as hard as I could. "Mom, when we were born, did you have some kind of premonition that we'd be going to Paris someday? You gave us such nice French names — Nicole and Nina. We'll feel right at home."

Everyone laughed except Ted. He was pouting. "What about me? "How do I make Ted sound French? I'll feel left out."

Nicole leaned over and kissed him. "No you won't. While we're in Paris, Nina and I will call you Pierre."

I could tell by the look in their eyes that they were happy together, and I was glad for them. It crossed my mind again, that phrase I was hearing so much lately: ". . . . a lot in common." It was true for Sandi and John and it was true for Nicole and Ted, too.

Nicole loved the bracelet, and she loved and laughed over the fun fur coat Mom and Dad gave her. "Should I wear it over my bathing suit?"

"Darling girl," Mom said. "You know perfectly well they're showing fall and winter things now — in fact, since the beginning of August. I've been hoping Nina would take some interest in school clothes, ride to Hyannis with me, or to Boston some weekday with your father, but she has been just . . . so busy."

I hoped Nicole wouldn't notice Mom's disapproving look at me, but she did.

"Busy with what, Neen? Painting, I hope. Have any new things to show us?"

I shook my head from side to side. "Mom means I've been busy with Ben. Ben is a boy I met this summer. I've been going out with him a lot."

Mom's eyes rolled back in her head. "A lot is right. Every day, every night. He's a perfectly nice boy, of course, but Nina hasn't had a min-

ute to herself. She hardly sees her friends, and
— Nina, have you done anything on your art?
I haven't seen anything."

Why did she have to bring it up now? It
was supposed to be a celebration — a reunion
and Nicole's birthday party.

"I'm doing okay," I mumbled. "Let's talk
about something else. For instance, how are
all your kids? Tell us about them, tell us all
about your work."

That was a surefire way of getting the attention off me. Both Nicole and Ted loved the
kids they worked with. They always had so
many stories to tell, some of them sad, some of
them success stories. The kids they worked
with were brain-damaged, some very severely.

After dinner and before Ben came over to
pick me up, Nicole and I had a few minutes
alone. "This Ben — is it serious, Nina?"

I looked her straight in the eye. "Sort of,
yes. I love him, or at least I think I do. I've
never felt this way about anyone before. He's
so nice, he really is, but Mom and Dad don't
appreciate him too much. They don't think
he's right for me because he's a Capie. Mom
says we don't have anything in common, and
we haven't any hope for a future together . . .
I don't know, Nicole, at this point, I just don't
know."

"Your first real love," she said quietly. "It's
wonderful and kind of awful, isn't it? I remember the way I felt about Bill Mayhew — do you
remember him?"

I tried to remember and couldn't. I shook

my head. "Well, I do," she said. "I'll never forget him. I don't think anyone ever forgets their very first love."

I looked at her. "What are you saying? That Ben will be just a memory someday? He'll be out of my life and I'll just . . ."

She reached over and touched my cheek. "I didn't mean that at all. I was just getting nostalgic, that's all. I'm not saying you shouldn't love Ben; I don't even know him, for heaven's sake. All I want to say, I guess, is get your priorities straight, Nina. You're sixteen and it's summer. Things can look different in the winter."

"I'm trying to, Nicole," I said, and my voice was kind of shaky. "That's exactly what I'm trying to do — sort out everything. I'm glad you're here. I missed you. Grantham has never been the same since you got married, you know. In fact, this summer is not at all like it used be."

"I know what you mean," she said softly. "It's hard sometimes, isn't it? Not being little girls anymore?"

I smiled at her. "Without a care in the world?"

She wrinkled her nose at me. "That's what I mean."

Ben arrived then, and I saw him get out of the truck and come up the steps to the porch. "Come on," I told Nicole, "I want you to meet him. Just you — Ben gets nervous when he has to come in and make small talk with Mom and Dad; he's really shy."

She let me lead her to the porch, and she was nice with Ben; he seemed to like her, too. "You look like Nina," he told her.

Nicole's laughter was like mine, too, I noticed. "No, Ben — you're wrong. Nina looks like *me*. I'm the oldest."

She was smiling when Ben and I headed for the porch, and she said: "We'll catch up with each other tomorrow on the beach, Nina. I can't *wait* for the beach."

But when I looked back, just before we drove away, I saw that Nicole was frowning after us. Like Mom, like Olivia, like Sandi. It seemed everyone was worried about me.

I couldn't really blame them. I was worried about me, too.

I knew when I walked into Ben's house on Monday night that they had gone to a lot of trouble for me. The kids had strung crepe paper from front door to kitchen door, and there were balloons tied to every available doorknob and curtain rod. I had to smile. "Hey, it's not my birthday."

"We know," Cindy said importantly. "It's your Thank-You Day — that's what Ma said."

Mrs. Turner was all dressed up. I hadn't realized how pretty she was, but a soft blue sweater and a touch of makeup helped to brighten her tired face. She even had earrings on.

The kitchen table was laden with food, and in the middle was a huge bouquet of daisies mixed with black-eyed Susans.

Susan was the new baby's name.

"Oh, let me hold her," I said, taking the infant from Mrs. Turner's arms. "Look how big she is."

The first time I had seen the baby when they brought her home from the hospital, I had been afraid to touch her. She was the tiniest thing I had ever seen. But now she didn't look too delicate; her cheeks were plump, and she was smiling at me.

"She just has gas," Cindy said. "But sometimes she really does smile. At me."

I looked at the eight-year-old and wondered — if Ben and I did get married and I was around all the time — if Cindy would ever relent and like me. I looked at her again, and she squinched up her nose at me. I doubted it.

"Lobster stew," Mrs. Turner said, pointing to a huge urn, steam rising from it. "Ben says you love lobster. And I baked a nice bass. Mr. Turner caught it special over at Salt Pond."

All the kids stood around beaming, proud of their mother, proud that they were all dressed up in their best shorts and shirts. I wanted to cry.

"And potato salad and boiled potatoes, too. Little bit of everything, Nina. Hope you're good and hungry."

I wasn't, but I nodded vigorously. "Oh, yes, I am. And everything looks wonderful. You really outdid yourself."

She nodded, pleased, and gave me one of her rare smiles. Now I could see, even with the lipstick and the touch of blue eyeshadow, she looked tired.

Baby Susan squirmed in my arms and I held her closer. She smelled like sour milk and baby powder, but I didn't mind it — I liked the smell, in fact. She was a beautiful baby, healthy and dark-haired, and warm in my arms. If I married Ben, maybe our first baby would look like Susan.

Even Mr. Turner was all spruced up, his leathery face less grim, and he talked, if not to me, to the children. They answered him respectfully, a bit fearfully, as if he were a stranger.

Mrs. Turner felt she had to explain, I guess. "Paul's not around most of the time. I have to do most of the scolding and raising, but they love their father, don't you see?"

It was a nice dinner, a nice thing for them to do, and I tried very hard to be nice, too. I commented on practically every bite I took, and it was easy to say flattering things because the food was wonderful. It occurred to me that most of the dishes were shellfish, or regular fish, items Mr. Turner could catch for himself or get free. It stood to reason, though. With all those mouths to feed, it had to be hard.

Maybe Mrs. Turner read my mind, or maybe it was the subject she most often thought about. As we were clearing the table (Ben and his father and the kids leaving us in the kitchen together), she said, "I suppose it's a hard life." She pushed back a strand of gray-streaked hair. "But I tell myself I've got the best kids, the best man in Grantham, and there's always food on the table. What more should anyone ask for?"

I wanted to answer her, wanted to tell her how much more I wanted, but she said bluntly, "Do you think you'll marry Ben?"

I was glad that I had an armload of dishes and I could busy myself stacking them near the sink.

"I'm not sure, Mrs. Turner," I said. "I care for Ben so much, but getting married — well, that's not exactly what I had planned. Not at seventeen, anyway."

She nodded, her expression serious.

"It's something to think hard about, that's sure. I was your age when I married Paul. Then Ben came along, and I thought for a long time he was the only child I'd ever have. I was going to open a little store . . ."

She stopped talking abruptly and turned on the faucet full force.

I was curious. "What kind of store, Mrs. Turner?"

"Oh," she said in an offhand way, "just a little one, a card store mostly, and souvenirs. I always liked pretty greeting cards. Even now I tell Paul and Ben — just get me a nice card for my birthday, that's all I want. Anyway, I thought I could make a go of it. I was always kind of good with numbers in school, and that's important in a small business. . . ." She put her head down and sighed. "No need for a card shop in Grantham anymore — too many shops now, the streets so crowded and all."

"I guess so," I said, looking at Ben's mother in a new way.

"Then the babies started to come," she continued. "I didn't have time to think much about a store."

She glanced at me, gave me a tiny smile. "I used to be a big reader."

I smiled, too, and I hoped, for her sake, I didn't look too sad.

"Ben showed me the picture you drew. You're good at it."

I was pleased *and* very surprised.

"Thank you. I love . . . drawing."

She gave a long, hard sigh, and the suds in the sink quivered.

"It's nice to have a hobby. I told Ben he should encourage you to keep at it after you're married. You'll be alone lots of times, married to a fisherman. Nice to have something to do until the babies start coming. After that . . . well, you won't have much time for hobbies. The most I do now is clip coupons out of the papers and magazines Ben brings home for me. It saves me lots of money at the checkout. I guess you could call coupons my hobby now."

Every word she said made me more depressed. And she called my art a hobby. Would she understand that it wasn't, that it was my work, work I loved? Hobbies were what my mother had, a million of them. Hobbies were things you did for fun, but you didn't take seriously.

If I looked ahead into the future, could I see myself clipping food coupons out of the evening paper, satisfied to be saving pennies? It was a terrible, terrible thought.

Mrs. Turner had given me an apron to wear "so you won't spoil your beautiful dress," and now, with the dishes done and the floor swept, I took off the apron and hung it on the hook in the hallway off the kitchen. When I turned, Mrs. Turner was standing there, looking at me, a dreamy smile on her face.

"It was nice, wasn't it, Nina?" she asked, as if I were her oldest friend. "The table set pretty, the flowers and all. Paul liked it, too, I could tell." She sighed. "I really should do it more often. Maybe put the kids to bed early, put out some candles. We used to do that sometimes."

I wanted to hug her. No wonder Ben loved his mother so much. I also wanted to run out of the too-small, shabby house, and away from all those dark-eyed, beautiful children.

I insisted on helping her put the kids to bed. She protested. "You've done enough. You shouldn't have even helped with the dishes. You *are* the guest."

I made a face. "I want to," I said firmly. "You go sit in the living room with Paul — I mean, with Mr. Turner. You worked so hard making the dinner. Ben and I will take care of everything."

She smiled gratefully and went to join her husband.

All the kids, including Cindy, were good.

Even Billy was helpful, undressing little Bobby and putting on his pajamas. I sat with them for a while and talked to them, and when they begged for a story, I told them one, the only one I could remember: Pinocchio, and how when he told a lie his nose grew. They loved it. And for a moment I loved every one of those kids. I felt as if I was really a part of this family. Ben's family.

Next summer I really could be.

Chapter
Seventeen

Dad had said that we'd be leaving Grantham on Wednesday morning, as usual, at the crack of dawn. This would be my last day with Ben. He surprised me last night when he told me he was taking the day off from fishing.

"Pate said I had it coming," he'd told me in a pleased voice. "Said I did a fair-to-middlin' job all summer." He laughed. "That's Pate-talk for great. Anyway, I've got a full tank of gas, and I thought we'd take a ride to Nauset Beach, pack a lunch, have a picnic. How does that sound, Nina? I know you like the beach."

I reached over and squeezed his hand. "I'd say that sounds like a fair-to-middlin' idea, Ben."

Now we were on our way to Orleans and Nauset. It was a beautiful day, all blue and gold with just a hint of autumn cool in the air. I sighed.

"Summer's over, Ben. It went so fast, didn't it? I always feel sad after Labor Day; I hate for it to end." I looked up at him and really did feel a deep sadness as our eyes met briefly. "And Grantham's so deserted already; everyone's gone home."

His mouth twisted. "Not everyone. And I'll be some sorry to see *you* go, but the truth is I like Grantham like this. We all do — can't help feeling that way, I guess. Seems like the town's in a mess during the summer, so much traffic, too many people . . ."

He sounded just like his mother. "No offense, Nina — I didn't mean you or your folks."

For some reason I thought of Enoch Webb in the pharmacy. "Love to see you summer girls come down to brighten up the place . . ." Mr. Webb had said that at the beginning of the summer, but I knew he liked to see us go, too. Everyone did, even Ben. It never changes, I thought. Maybe no one can ever erase that definite but invisible line that separates us; summer people and Capies.

Ben drove the old truck fast but sure over the road to Orleans, and I looked out the window at the neat houses and the pines that bordered the road. We passed only an occasional car, and I couldn't help but think of this same road when snow covered the ground. It would be so cold and empty — and, I thought, boring. What did people do for fun in the winter? I was going to ask, but I decided not to.

Nauset Beach is the best beach for miles around, or at least the waves are the most impressive, and I love the dunes. They looked like sculptures on the deserted beach. Beach grass, gray-green and silver, swayed in the ocean breeze. Ben handed me a blanket from the back of the truck, and before he picked up the heavy picnic basket, he bent down and took off his shoes and socks. I had to laugh. "You're learning," I said, but when his bare feet touched the sand I saw an expression of disgust cross his face. "Ben, I don't understand — if you love Grantham so much, how come you can't stand walking in sand? Isn't sand as much a part of Grantham as the ocean?"

He nodded, his eyes looking straight ahead as usual, at the water, at the spot where sky meets sea. "Ayuh, but we don't like laying around in it like you do. Maybe it has to do with the fact that we don't have that much time for it. I never could understand why folks come miles to lay around and splash in the water. Swimming wouldn't do me much good if our boat sank, Nina — not way out there where we go."

He thought I was frivolous for wanting a tan, loving to walk in the sand along the water's edge, riding the waves, laughing, playing games with my friends in the water.

We spread the blanket and weighted it down with the heavy basket. I pulled my sweatshirt off over my head, and then just stood for a minute in my white bikini, letting the sun warm me. "Maybe you don't love this, Ben," I said, "but I really do. I look forward to it all winter, just feeling the sun on my face, listening to the sounds of the ocean, smelling it."

I saw that he could agree with that. "Don't blame you," he said. "When I drive up to Boston with a load of fish, I can't wait to get back here. It's hard to understand how you people even breathe up there, all that bad air. Don't know what I'd do without the clean salt air. Do you know I can sniff out what kind of fish are running when we're out there? Cod's the easiest, but I can tell them all."

He looked proud and happy when he said that. "Can we walk for a while, Ben? I want to collect some shells to bring home with me; I meant to do that all week, but I forgot, I guess. I *always* bring shells home with me."

Did I sound very defensive? He was smiling at me, but I thought I saw a pitying look in his eyes, as if he were saying: "Poor little summer girl, has to go home to dirty old Boston and leave all this behind."

As we neared the water's edge, I could feel the sand shifting under my feet, just one small warning of the strong undertow at Nauset. I looked down and my eyes widened. "Look, Ben — what luck! A seahorse. Isn't it pretty?" I scooped it up in my hand, then flattened my palm and studied it. "I haven't found one of these for a long time."

Ben was bending down now, and when he straightened up I could tell he was holding something behind his back. I looked at him and grinned. "Oh, so you're trying to outdo me — what did you find, Ben?"

He wasn't smiling when he handed me the rusted soda can. He didn't say a word, but I knew the can was an indictment against tourists, summer people. "I'd never do that," I said quietly, but I resented it, resented *him*.

He made it worse. "Nauset is some nice when it's not all cluttered up with people. And look way out there, Nina," he said, pointing. "I'm pretty sure that's our boat, the *Catherine T.*"

In profile, with his chin lifted, his gaze fixed, his lips slightly parted, he looked more Indian than ever. I'd never said that to him. Now I did.

"Not Indian — Portuguese," he said. "My grandmother on my father's side was pure Portuguese. Lots of them down here, Nina, most of them are fishermen. Probably that's where I get it from. My ma was an Eldredge — that's old Cape Cod — so I've got it from both sides."

The sand ahead of us was smooth; near the water it was silver, and its wetness held our footprints for only a second or two.

"You really love what you do, Ben, don't you? I mean, you told me that, but you're really sure this is what you want to do all your life — live in Grantham and be a fisherman. The way you talked about Boston before: You don't like the city at all, do you?"

He looked at me sharply. "Nope, the city

makes me nervous. How about you? You really like all that noise and dirt and tall buildings?"

The day was not going very well, but at least — like it or not — I was learning more about Ben. "Sure I do. And Boston isn't just . . . well, what you said. There's so much more there, to do and see. Maybe you just haven't seen the good parts. You'll have to come up and let me take you around, show you my world."

He looked doubtful. "Sure, I'll be driving up sometimes. I couldn't stand not seeing you for too long. Maybe you can get your parents to come down here some weekends, too." He smiled and took my free hand. "We'll manage, Nina. We'll get to see each other."

I looked up at him and smiled. "Of course we will. The Cape isn't that far from my house." I tugged at his hand. "Let's go back to the blanket, Ben. I know it isn't even close to noon yet, but I'm starving. The beach always gives me the hungries."

He laughed. "Me, too — I'll race you back."

By the time we got back I was panting, and we were both laughing, acting like starving fiends, rummaging in the basket and grabbing at sandwiches. My bad mood disappeared, and I decided I wasn't going to spoil the rest of the day — my last day with Ben — with talk that I knew would upset me. Besides, it was too beautiful a day; the sun was very warm now, but there was a constant cooling breeze, too — perfect.

For someone who hated to loll around the beach, Ben adjusted very well. I was pleased with him. He was in a good mood, and then a tender one, writing words on my bare back with suntan oil and making me guess what they were. I got to recognize the word "love" quickly because he repeated that one so often.

There was no one to see us, so we kissed quite a lot as the afternoon grew late and the sun started to get low. A sense of urgency seemed to pull us together, and we sat up, watching the tide come in, and cuddled close.

He was looking at me intensely, a dark, warm stare that I could feel like breath on my face. We didn't have very much time now; I would have to get back soon. Dad and Mom had insisted I join them for dinner at The Colony — our farewell-to-Grantham dinner.

I could feel his question building, too; I knew what he was going to ask me.

"You never gave me an answer, Nina. You've just said 'maybe.' Will you tell me now — are you going to marry me next June?"

I didn't have any time left to think about it, worry about it. I knew I would have to give him my answer right now.

It was so hard because just a short time before I had been in his arms, kissing him, feeling so strongly the current that had been there right from the start. How could I tell him without hurting him that I loved him but that I couldn't marry him? Would he understand now what he couldn't understand before?

"Ben — I have to be honest. I'm being honest when I say I've never felt this way about anyone ever before. Just being with you has been so wonderful, and I love so many things about you . . . oh, I don't know . . . *everything* about you. I understand how much you care about your family, your life here, being a fisherman; and I love you for those things. That's why I hope you can understand about my dreams, too, the way I feel about my work."

I wasn't really looking at him, but I could feel him tense up.

"That's what I've tried to explain before — my art isn't just a pastime, a hobby that I turn to when there's nothing better to do, although I've really neglected it this summer. You want to be the best at what you do, right? Well, I do, too. I'm lucky enough to have parents and friends who are offering me the chance to study and learn from the great artists. I can't let that chance go, Ben, and I would be if I got married too early — to anyone. There is so much I have to do and see and learn before I can even think about marriage. Can you understand? I love you, Ben, but . . ."

"It's too dull down here for you, Nina. I'm too dull, I guess."

I turned and touched his face. "No! It's not that. Ben — didn't you listen to me?"

He stood up and faced the ocean; his hands were jammed into his back pockets, and his head was lowered. His voice was deep and rough.

"I don't give up that easy, Nina," he said, not looking at me. "I'll be coming up to Boston regular, and I'm going to write to you, too. I love you, and maybe by next summer that will be more important to you than going off to Paris, France."

He *had* listened to me before; I hadn't even mentioned Paris today.

"I'm going to Paris next summer, Ben," I said quietly. "I have to." I knew I couldn't give him false hope.

He still stood there, not looking at me. "Ayuh, but you'll come back to Boston after that, won't you?"

"Sure . . . but . . ."

"The summer after next, maybe. I won't stop loving you. How can I? You're the first girl I ever loved — I won't forget."

I thought of Nicole and what she had said about first loves.

"I won't forget either, Ben," I said, getting up to stand beside him. "I know that for sure — I won't ever forget you."

He was silent for a long time. Probably it was only a trick of the light, but for a moment Ben looked exactly like his father, his eyelids lowered secretively, his lips pressed tight together. But then that spell was broken, when he whirled suddenly and put his arms around me, lifted me, and swung me around.

"Nope, I won't stop trying, Nina. So don't be surprised when you find me standing on your doorstep up there in Boston, or when you get a letter from me every week. I'm not much for letter-writing, but maybe it will give me something to do on winter nights while I'm waiting."

I was breathless when he released me, but I said, "I'll write you back, Ben — I promise. And maybe I can talk Mom and Dad into spending Thanksgiving down here."

He nodded, and his face was relaxed now. "Your folks are okay — ayuh, your dad's all right — I like him."

"Oh, Ben," I whispered, feeling the wetness in my eyes, "I wish —"

He wouldn't let me finish. "Don't forget your seashore, Nina — it's a beauty. Come on, help me fold the blanket. It's getting some cold down here."

I shivered, but it wasn't from the damp-cool breeze. "It was the best summer of my life, Ben Turner."

He smiled at me, his brown eyes warm. "Ayuh — me, too, Nina. The best summer of my life."

We drove in near-silence, but it wasn't a strained silence. When we got to my house, he leaned over and kissed me long and hard, not caring that Dad was puttering around by the garage. "So long, Nina girl," he said softly, and I knew he didn't want me to say good-bye.

"So long, Ben. I'll be seeing you."

He was already in driving position, and he didn't look at me as I opened the truck door, but I heard him say, very softly, "Ayuh."

He drove away, and I walked up the steps and sat down in the rocker at the farthest end of the porch. I thought maybe I would cry, but I didn't. For some reason I didn't feel like crying.

Chapter Eighteen

I pretended to be very sleepy. At barely seven in the morning it was as good an excuse as any not to have to make conversation with Mom and Dad. I helped pack the car and then sat on the porch while Dad locked the doors, front and back. The rockers had all been stored in the garage a few moments before, so I sat on the top step, my head cradled in my arms. I didn't feel like talking to anyone.

"Well, good morning, Ross," I heard Mom say cheerily. "I thought everyone had gone back to Boston. In fact, we're just about on our way."

I'd thought so, too. What was Ross doing here so early? I didn't feel like talking to him. Besides, I knew I probably looked terrible. If I had brushed my teeth and hair when I got up, that's about all I had done.

I looked up at him and then decided the least I could do was look a little bit alive. It was impolite not to at least give him a little smile, a little hello.

"Hi, Ross. What are you doing up so early?"

He shrugged and smiled at the same time. "Same thing you are, I guess. My mother likes to wait at least a couple of days after Labor Day, to avoid the traffic, she says."

"My father, too. I just think he likes to stretch out the summer as long as he can."

He sat down beside me and stretched out his legs. Ross did have very long legs. In tan corduroys they looked endless. He smelled good, too, like peppermint and sunshine.

"Well, it's over," he said mildly.

I glanced at him quickly.

"What's over?"

He looked at me out of the corner of his eye.

"Summer's over," he said. "Haven't you noticed?"

His voice was teasing, but I couldn't answer him the same way. I just nodded.

"It's really beautiful here," he said. "Guess I hate to leave, too. Probably won't get down next summer."

"How come?" I asked politely, but I was thinking. All these years, Sandi and Ross and John, Amy and Bunny and me. Everything was changed. Nothing was the same anymore.

"I'm going to be working next summer. In

Boston. In my father's store." He sighed. "He wants me to learn the business."

"Oh, Ross," I said, suddenly sympathetic. "Who wants to spend the summer cooped up in a store? Even if that store is the most beautiful one on Newbury Street." Mr. Bradford owns The Glass Menagerie, where they sell the finest china — Wedgewood and Havilland — and crystals and . . . well, everything gorgeous you can think of.

But he didn't seem to need my sympathy. "Only for *half* the summer," he said, and I detected a slyness in his voice.

"Then what?" I asked, checking to see if Dad and Mom were ready to roll. They weren't. In fact, they looked very busy. Suspiciously busy. Giving me time with Ross, that's what they were doing.

"Then I'll be a traveling a little. Might go to London for a couple weeks."

I tried to catch Mom's eye so I could give her a dirty look. I could just hear her: "Oh, yes — Nina will be going to Paris next summer. Our friends, the Yateses, have arranged it all. . . ."

"That's great, Ross," I said. Did I sound too blah?

"Then maybe, if I have some time, to Paris. Maybe I'll look you up."

"Yes, do that, Ross," I said, making my voice as bright as I could.

Nicole, Ted, now Ross. Maybe I wouldn't have time to do my art in Paris, either.

185

He stood up and took a few steps away from me. He squinted up at the sun, then down at me. The sun was filtering through the morning fog.

"Of course, you never can tell," he said. "By next summer my plans may have changed. I'll let you know, okay?"

His hair was so smooth and blond. His eyes were very blue against the tan of his face. He moved farther away from me, at first backwards and then turning, he headed off down the driveway. I saw him lift his hand, probably to wave at me, but then he stopped and walked back and stood right in front of me.

"Listen, Nina, I was just wondering. It's none of my business but . . ." His next words came out in a rush. "Are you still all tied up?"

He didn't have to say Ben's name.

I shook my head slowly. "Uh uh. No, Ross, I'm not tied up."

I couldn't smile, but he did. He turned away again and started walking. He stopped one more time.

"Hey, Nina. Around Valentine's Day, maybe you'll get some interesting mail."

He had that old Dennis the Menace look on his face. This time I did smile.

"I'm looking forward to it," I said. "But this time, Ross — put enough stamps on it."

He waved without turning around, and then he disappeared around the corner.

Good-bye, Ross, I thought. Good-bye, Ben.

Moments later, as we drove through Grantham and passed the statue of old Josiah, I took one long last look and said it again.

Good-bye, Ben. Good-bye, summer. I knew it had probably been the most important one of my life.